The Pat Hobby Stories

F. Scott Fitzgerald

ALMA CLASSICS LTD
London House
243-253 Lower Mortlake Road
Richmond
Surrey TW9 2LL
United Kingdom
www.almaclassics.com

The Pat Hobby Stories first published in volume form in 1962
This edition first published by Alma Books Ltd in 2014

Notes © Alma Classics Ltd
Extra Material © Richard Parker

Printed and bound by CPI Group (UK) Ltd, Croydon, CR0 4YY

ISBN: 978-1-84749-385-9

Contents

Other books by F. SCOTT FITZGERALD
published by Alma Classics

All the Sad Young Men

Basil and Josephine

Babylon Revisited and Other Stories

The Beautiful and Damned

Flappers and Philosophers

The Great Gatsby

The Last of the Belles and Other Stories

The Last Tycoon

The Love Boat and Other Stories

Tales of the Jazz Age

Tender Is the Night

This Side of Paradise

F. Scott Fitzgerald (1896–1940)

Edward Fitzgerald,
Fitzgerald's father

Mary McQuillan Fitzgerald,
Fitzgerald's mother

Ginevra King

Zelda Fitzgerald

The Fitzgeralds' house in Montgomery, Alabama

The Fitzgeralds' grave in Rockville, Maryland,
inscribed with the closing line from *The Great Gatsby*

The cover of the January 1940 issue of *Esquire*,
which contained the first Pat Hobby story

The Pat Hobby Stories

Pat Hobby's Christmas Wish

1

I T WAS CHRISTMAS EVE in the studio. By eleven o'clock in the morning, Santa Claus had called on most of the huge population according to each one's deserts.

Sumptuous gifts from producers to stars, and from agents to producers, arrived at offices and studio bungalows; on every stage one heard of the roguish gifts of casts to directors or directors to casts; champagne had gone out from publicity office to the press. And tips of fifties, tens and fives from producers, directors and writers fell like manna upon the white-collar class.

In this sort of transaction there were exceptions. Pat Hobby, for example, who knew the game from twenty years' experience, had had the idea of getting rid of his secretary the day before. They were sending over a new one any minute – but she would scarcely expect a present the first day.

Waiting for her, he walked the corridor, glancing into open offices for signs of life. He stopped to chat with Joe Hopper from the scenario department.

"Not like the old days," he mourned. "Then there was a bottle on every desk."

"There're a few around."

"Not many." Pat sighed. "And afterwards we'd run a picture – made up out of cutting-room scraps."

"I've heard. All the suppressed stuff," said Hopper.

Pat nodded, his eyes glistening.

"Oh, it was juicy. You darned near ripped your guts laughing…"

He broke off as the sight of a woman, pad in hand, entering his office down the hall recalled him to the sorry present.

"Gooddorf has me working over the holiday," he complained bitterly.

"I wouldn't do it."

"I wouldn't either except my four weeks are up next Friday, and if I bucked him he wouldn't extend me."

As he turned away, Hopper knew that Pat was not being extended anyhow. He had been hired to script an old-fashioned horse opera, and the boys who were "writing behind him" – that is working over his stuff – said that all of it was old and some didn't make sense.

"I'm Miss Kagle," said Pat's new secretary.

She was about thirty-six, handsome, faded, tired, efficient. She went to the typewriter, examined it, sat down and burst into sobs.

Pat started. Self-control, from below anyhow, was the rule around here. Wasn't it bad enough to be working on Christmas Eve? Well – less bad than not working at all. He walked over and shut the door – someone might suspect him of insulting the girl.

"Cheer up," he advised her. "This is Christmas."

Her burst of emotion had died away. She sat upright now, choking and wiping her eyes.

"Nothing's as bad as it seems," he assured her unconvincingly. "What's it, anyhow? They going to lay you off?"

She shook her head, did a sniffle to end sniffles and opened her notebook.

"Who you been working for?"

She answered between suddenly gritted teeth.

"Mr Harry Gooddorf."

Pat widened his permanently bloodshot eyes. Now he remembered he had seen her in Harry's outer office.

"Since 1921. Eighteen years. And yesterday he sent me back to the department. He said I depressed him – I reminded him he was getting on." Her face was grim. "That isn't the way he talked after hours eighteen years ago."

"Yeah, he was a skirt-chaser then," said Pat.

"I should have done something then when I had the chance."

Pat felt righteous stirrings.

"Breach of promise? That's no angle!"

"But I had something to clinch it. Something bigger than breach of promise. I still have too. But then, you see, I thought I was in love with him." She brooded for a moment. "Do you want to dictate something now?"

Pat remembered his job and opened a script.

"It's an insert," he began. "Scene 114 A."

Pat paced the office.

"Ext. Long Shot of the Plains," he decreed. "Buck and Mexicans approaching the hyacenda."

"The what?"

5

"The hyacenda – the ranch house." He looked at her reproachfully. "114 B. Two Shot: Buck and Pedro. Buck: 'The dirty son of a bitch. I'll tear his guts out!'"

Miss Kagle looked up, startled.

"You want me to write that down?"

"Sure."

"It won't get by."

"I'm writing this. Of course, it won't get by. But if I put 'you rat', the scene won't have any force."

"But won't somebody have to change it to 'you rat'?"

He glared at her – he didn't want to change secretaries every day.

"Harry Gooddorf can worry about that."

"Are you working for Mr Gooddorf?" Miss Kagle asked in alarm.

"Until he throws me out."

"I shouldn't have said—"

"Don't worry," he assured her. "He's no pal of mine any more. Not at three fifty a week, when I used to get two thousand... Where was I?"

He paced the floor again, repeating his last line aloud with relish. But now it seemed to apply not to a personage of the story but to Harry Gooddorf. Suddenly he stood still, lost in thought. "Say, what is it you got on him? You know where the body is buried?"

"That's too true to be funny."

"He knock somebody off?"

"Mr Hobby, I'm sorry I ever opened my mouth."

"Just call me Pat. What's your first name?"

"Helen."

"Married?"

"Not now."

"Well, listen Helen: what do you say we have dinner?"

2

O N THE AFTERNOON OF CHRISTMAS DAY, he was still trying to get the secret out of her. They had the studio almost to themselves – only a skeleton staff of technical men dotted the walks and the commissary. They had exchanged Christmas presents. Pat gave her a five-dollar bill, Helen bought him a white linen handkerchief. Very well he could remember the day when many dozen such handkerchiefs had been his Christmas harvest.

The script was progressing at a snail's pace, but their friendship had considerably ripened. Her secret, he considered, was a very valuable asset, and he wondered how many careers had turned on just such an asset. Some, he felt sure, had been thus raised to affluence. Why, it was almost as good as being in the family, and he pictured an imaginary conversation with Harry Gooddorf.

"Harry, it's this way. I don't think my experience is being made use of. It's the young squirts who ought to do the writing – I ought to do more supervising."

"Or?"

"Or else," said Pat firmly.

He was in the midst of his daydream when Harry Gooddorf unexpectedly walked in.

"Merry Christmas, Pat," he said jovially. His smile was less robust when he saw Helen: "Oh, hello Helen – didn't know you and Pat had got together. I sent you a remembrance over to the script department."

"You shouldn't have done that."

Harry turned swiftly to Pat.

"The boss is on my neck," he said. "I've got to have a finished script Thursday."

"Well, here I am," said Pat. "You'll have it. Did I ever fail you?"

"Usually," said Harry. "Usually."

He seemed about to add more when a call boy entered with an envelope and handed it to Helen Kagle – whereupon Harry turned and hurried out.

"He'd better get out!" burst forth Miss Kagle, after opening the envelope. "Ten bucks – just *ten bucks* – from an executive – after eighteen years."

It was Pat's chance. Sitting on her desk, he told her his plan.

"It's soft jobs for you and me," he said. "You the head of a script department, me an associate producer. We're on the gravy train for life – no more writing – no more pounding the keys. We might even... we might even... if things go good we could get married."

She hesitated a long time. When she put a fresh sheet in the typewriter, Pat feared he had lost.

"I can write it from memory," she said. "This was a letter he typed *himself* on February 3rd, 1921. He sealed it and gave it to me to mail – but there was a blonde he was interested in, and I wondered why he should be so secret about a letter."

Helen had been typing as she talked, and now she handed Pat a note.

> *To Will Bronson*
> *First National Studios*
> *Personal*

Dear Bill:

We killed Taylor. We should have cracked down on him sooner. So why not shut up.

> *Yours, Harry*

Pat stared at it, stunned.

"Get it?" Helen said. "On February 1st, 1921, somebody knocked off William Desmond Taylor, the director. And they've never found out who."

3

FOR EIGHTEEN YEARS she had kept the original note, envelope and all. She had sent only a copy to Bronson, tracing Harry Gooddorf's signature.

"Baby, we're set!" said Pat. "I always thought it was a *girl* got Taylor."

He was so elated that he opened a drawer and brought forth a half-pint of whiskey. Then, with an afterthought, he demanded:

"Is it in a safe place?"

"You bet it is. He'd never guess where."

"Baby, we've got him!"

Cash, cars, girls, swimming pools swam in a glittering montage before Pat's eye.

He folded the note, put it in his pocket, took another drink and reached for his hat.

"You going to see him now?" Helen demanded in some alarm. "Hey, wait till I get off the lot. *I* don't want to get murdered."

"Don't worry! Listen, I'll meet you in The Muncherie at Fifth and La Brea – in one hour."

As he walked to Gooddorf's office, he decided to mention no facts or names within the walls of the studio. Back in the brief period when he had headed a scenario department, Pat had conceived a plan to put a Dictaphone in every writer's office. Thus their loyalty to the studio executives could be checked several times a day.

The idea had been laughed at. But later, when he had been "reduced back to a writer", he often wondered if his plan was secretly followed. Perhaps some indiscreet remark of his own was responsible for the doghouse where he had been interred for the past decade. So it was with the idea of concealed Dictaphones in mind, Dictaphones which could be turned on by the pressure of a toe, that he entered Harry Gooddorf's office.

"Harry…" he chose his words carefully, "do you remember the night of February 1st, 1921?"

Somewhat flabbergasted, Gooddorf leant back in his swivel chair.

"*What?*"

"Try and think. It's something very important to you."

Pat's expression as he watched his friend was that of an anxious undertaker.

"February 1st, 1921." Gooddorf mused. "No. How could I remember? You think I keep a diary? I don't even know where I was then."

"You were right here in Hollywood."

"Probably. If you know, tell me."

"You'll remember."

"Let's see. I came out to the coast in 'Sixteen. I was with Biograph* till 1920. Was I making some comedies? That's it. I was making a piece called *Knuckleduster* – on location."

"You weren't always on location. You were in town February 1st."

"What is this?" Gooddorf demanded. "The third degree?"

"No – but I've got some information about your doings on that date."

Gooddorf's face reddened; for a moment it looked as if he were going to throw Pat out of the room – then suddenly he gasped, licked his lips and stared at his desk.

"Oh," he said and, after a minute: "But I don't see what business it is of yours."

"It's the business of every decent man."

"Since when have you been decent?"

"All my life," said Pat. "And, even if I haven't, I never did anything like that."

"My foot!" said Harry contemptuously. "*You* showing up here with a halo! Anyhow, what's the evidence? You'd think you had a written confession. It's all forgotten long ago."

"Not in the memory of decent men," said Pat. "And as for a written confession – I've got it."

"I doubt you. And I doubt if it would stand in any court. You've been taken in."

"I've seen it," said Pat with growing confidence. "And it's enough to hang you."

"Well, by God, if there's any publicity I'll run you out of town."

"You'll run *me* out of town."

"I don't want any publicity."

"Then I think you'd better come along with me. Without talking to anybody."

"Where are we going?"

"I know a bar where we can be alone."

The Muncherie was in fact deserted, save for the bartender and Helen Kagle, who sat at a table, jumpy with alarm. Seeing her, Gooddorf's expression changed to one of infinite reproach.

"This is a hell of a Christmas," he said, "with my family expecting me home an hour ago. I want to know the idea. You say you've got something in my writing."

Pat took the paper from his pocket and read the date aloud. Then he looked up hastily:

"This is just a copy, so don't try and snatch it."

He knew the technique of such scenes as this. When the vogue for Westerns had temporarily subsided he had sweated over many an orgy of crime.

"To William Bronson, Dear Bill: We killed Taylor. We should have cracked down on him sooner. So why not shut up. Yours, Harry."

Pat paused. "You wrote this on February 3rd, 1921."

Silence. Gooddorf turned to Helen Kagle.

"Did *you* do this? Did I dictate that to you?"

"No," she admitted in an awed voice. "You wrote it yourself. I opened the letter."

"I see. Well, what do you want?"

"Plenty," said Pat, and found himself pleased with the sound of the word.

"What exactly?"

Pat launched into the description of a career suitable to a man of forty-nine. A glowing career. It expanded rapidly in beauty and power during the time it took him to drink three large whiskeys. But one demand he returned to again and again.

He wanted to be made a producer tomorrow.

"Why tomorrow?" demanded Gooddorf. "Can't it wait?"

There were sudden tears in Pat's eyes – real tears.

"This is Christmas," he said. "It's my Christmas wish. I've had a hell of a time. I've waited so long."

Gooddorf got to his feet suddenly.

"Nope," he said. "I won't make you a producer. I couldn't do it in fairness to the company. I'd rather stand trial."

Pat's mouth fell open.

"What? You won't?"

"Not a chance. I'd rather swing."

He turned away, his face set, and started towards the door.

"All right!" Pat called after him. "It's your last chance."

Suddenly he was amazed to see Helen Kagle spring up and run after Gooddorf – try to throw her arms around him.

"Don't worry!" she cried. "I'll tear it up, Harry! It was a joke, Harry..."

Her voice trailed off rather abruptly. She had discovered that Gooddorf was shaking with laughter.

"What's the joke?" she demanded, growing angry again. "Do you think I haven't got it?"

"Oh, you've got it all right," Gooddorf howled. "You've got it – but it isn't what you think it is."

He came back to the table, sat down and addressed Pat.

"Do you know what I thought that date meant? I thought maybe it was the date Helen and I first fell for each other. That's what I thought. And I thought she was going to raise Cain about it. I thought she was nuts. She's been married twice since then, and so have I."

"That doesn't explain the note," said Pat sternly but with a sinky feeling. "You admit you killed Taylor."

Gooddorf nodded.

"I still think a lot of us did," he said. "We were a wild crowd – Taylor and Bronson and me and half the boys in the big money. So a bunch of us got together in an agreement to go slow. The country was waiting for somebody to hang. We tried to get Taylor to watch his step, but he wouldn't. So instead of cracking down on him, we let him 'go the pace'. And some rat shot him – who did it I don't know."

He stood up.

"Like somebody should have cracked down on *you*, Pat. But you were an amusing guy in those days, and besides, we were all too busy."

Pat sniffled suddenly.

"I've *been* cracked down on," he said. "Plenty."

"But too late," said Gooddorf, and added, "you've probably got a new Christmas wish by now, and I'll grant it to you. I won't say anything about this afternoon."

When he had gone, Pat and Helen sat in silence. Presently Pat took out the note again and looked it over.

"'So why not shut up?'" he read aloud. "He didn't explain that."

"Why *not* shut up?" Helen said.

A Man in the Way

1

P AT HOBBY COULD ALWAYS GET ON THE LOT. He had
worked there fifteen years on and off – chiefly off during
the past five – and most of the studio police knew him. If tough
customers on watch asked to see his studio card, he could get in
by phoning Lou, the bookie. For Lou also, the studio had been
home for many years.

Pat was forty-nine. He was a writer, but he had never written
much, nor even read all the "originals" he worked from, because it
made his head bang to read much. But the good old silent days you
got somebody's plot and a smart secretary and gulped Benzedrine
"structure" at her six or eight hours every week. The director took
care of the gags. After talkies came he always teamed up with some
man who wrote dialogue. Some young man who liked to work.

"I've got a list of credits second to none," he told Jack Berners.
"All I need is an idea and to work with somebody who isn't all wet."

He had buttonholed Jack outside the production office as Jack
was going to lunch, and they walked together in the direction of
the commissary.

"You bring *me* an idea," said Jack Berners. "Things are tight.
We can't put a man on salary unless he's got an idea."

"How can you get ideas off salary?" Pat demanded – then he added hastily: "Anyhow I got the germ of an idea that I could be telling you all about at lunch."

Something might come to him at lunch. There was Baer's notion about the boy scout. But Jack said cheerfully:

"I've got a date for lunch, Pat. Write it out and send it around, eh?"

He felt cruel, because he knew Pat couldn't write anything out, but he was having story trouble himself. The war had just broken out and every producer on the lot wanted to end their current stories with the hero going to war. And Jack Berners felt he had thought of that first for his production.

"So write it out, eh?"

When Pat didn't answer, Jack looked at him – he saw a sort of whipped misery in Pat's eye that reminded him of his own father. Pat had been in the money before Jack was out of college – with three cars and a chicken over every garage. Now his clothes looked as if he'd been standing at Hollywood and Vine for three years.

"Scout around and talk to some of the writers on the lot," he said. "If you can get one of them interested in your idea, bring him up to see me."

"I hate to give an idea without money on the line," Pat brooded pessimistically. "These young squirts'll lift the shirt off your back."

They had reached the commissary door.

"Good luck, Pat. Anyhow we're not in Poland."

"Good *you're* not," said Pat under his breath. "They'd slit your gizzard."

Now what to do? He went up and wandered along the cell block of writers. Almost everyone had gone to lunch, and those who were in he didn't know. Always there were more and more unfamiliar faces. And he had thirty credits; he had been in the business, publicity and scriptwriting, for twenty years.

The last door in the line belonged to a man he didn't like. But he wanted a place to sit a minute, so with a knock he pushed it open. The man wasn't there – only a very pretty, frail-looking girl sat reading a book.

"I think he's left Hollywood," she said in answer to his question. "They gave me his office, but they forgot to put up my name."

"You a writer?" Pat asked in surprise.

"I work at it."

"You ought to get 'em to give you a test."

"No – I like writing."

"What's that you're reading?"

She showed him.

"Let me give you a tip," he said. "That's not the way to get the guts out of a book."

"Oh."

"I've been here for years – I'm Pat Hobby – and I *know*. Give the book to four of your friends to read it. Get them to tell you what stuck in their minds. Write it down and you've got a picture – see?"

The girl smiled.

"Well, that's very... very original advice, Mr Hobby."

"Pat Hobby," he said. "Can I wait here a minute? Man I came to see is at lunch."

He sat down across from her and picked up a copy of a photo magazine.

"Oh, just let me mark that," she said quickly.

He looked at the page which she checked. It showed paintings being boxed and carted away to safety from an art gallery in Europe.

"How'll you use it?" he said.

"Well, I thought it would be dramatic if there was an old man around while they were packing the pictures. A poor old man, trying to get a job helping them. But they can't use him – he's in the way – not even good cannon fodder. They want strong young people in the world. And it turns out he's the man who painted the pictures many years ago."

Pat considered.

"It's good, but I don't get it," he said.

"Oh, it's nothing, a short short maybe."

"Got any good picture ideas? I'm in with all the markets here."

"I'm under contract."

"Use another name."

Her phone rang.

"Yes, this is Pricilla Smith," the girl said.

After a minute she turned to Pat.

"Will you excuse me? This is a private call."

He got it and walked out, and along the corridor. Finding an office with no name on it, he went in and fell asleep on the couch.

2

L ATE THAT AFTERNOON HE RETURNED to Jack Berners's waiting rooms. He had an idea about a man who meets a girl in an office and he thinks she's a stenographer, but she turns out to be a writer. He engages her as a stenographer, though, and they start for the South Seas. It was a beginning, it was something to tell Jack, he thought – and, picturing Pricilla Smith, he refurbished some old business he hadn't seen used for years.

He became quite excited about it – felt quite young for a moment – and walked up and down the waiting room mentally rehearsing the first sequence. "So here we have a situation like *It Happened One Night* – only *new*. I see Hedy Lamarr..."*

Oh, he knew how to talk to these boys if he could get to them with something to say.

"Mr Berners still busy?" he asked for the fifth time.

"Oh, yes, Mr Hobby. Mr Bill Costello and Mr Bach are in there."

He thought quickly. It was half-past five. In the old days he had just busted in sometimes and sold an idea, an idea good for a couple of grand, because it was just the moment when they were very tired of what they were doing at present.

He walked innocently out and to another door in the hall. He knew it led through a bathroom right into Jack Berners's office. Drawing a quick breath he plunged...

"...So that's the notion," he concluded after five minutes. "It's just a flash – nothing really worked out – but you could give me an office and a girl and I could have something on paper for you in three days."

Berners, Costello and Bach did not even have to look at each other. Berners spoke for them all as he said, firmly and gently:

"That's no idea, Pat. I can't put you on salary for that."

"Why don't you work it out further by yourself," suggested Bill Costello. "And then let's see it. We're looking for ideas – especially about the war."

"A man can think better on salary," said Pat.

There was silence. Costello and Bach had drunk with him, played poker with him, gone to the races with him. They'd honestly be glad to see him placed.

"The war, eh," he said gloomily. "Everything is war now, no matter how many credits a man has. Do you know what it makes me think of? It makes me think of a well-known painter in the discard. It's wartime and he's useless – just a man in the way" – he warmed to his conception of himself – "but all the time they're carting away *his own paintings* as the most valuable thing worth saving. And they won't even let me help. That's what it reminds me of."

There was again silence for a moment.

"That isn't a bad idea," said Bach thoughtfully. He turned to the others. "You know? In itself?"

Bill Costello nodded.

"Not bad at all. And I know where we could spot it. Right at the end of the fourth sequence. We just change old Ames to a painter."

Presently they talked money.

"I'll give you two weeks on it," said Berners to Pat. "At two fifty."

"Two fifty!" objected Pat. "Say, there was one time you paid me ten times that!"

"That was ten years ago," Jack reminded him. "Sorry. Best we can do now."

"You make me feel like that old painter—"

"Don't oversell it," said Jack, rising and smiling. "You're on the payroll."

Pat went out with a quick step and confidence in his eyes. Half a grand – that would take the pressure off for a month, and you could often stretch two weeks into three – sometimes four. He left the studio proudly through the front entrance, stopping at the liquor store for a half-pint to take back to his room.

By seven o'clock things were even better. Santa Anita* tomorrow, if he could get an advance. And tonight – something festive ought to be done tonight. With a sudden rush of pleasure, he went down to the phone in the lower hall, called the studio and asked for Miss Pricilla Smith's number. He hadn't met anyone so pretty for years...

In her apartment Pricilla Smith spoke rather firmly into the phone.

"I'm awfully sorry," she said, "but I couldn't possibly... No – and I'm tied up all the rest of the week."

As she hung up, Jack Berners spoke from the couch.

"Who was it?"

"Oh, some man who came in the office," she laughed, "and told me never to read the story I was working on."

"Shall I believe you?"

"You certainly shall. I'll even think of his name in a minute. But first I want to tell you about an idea I had this morning. I was looking at a photo in a magazine where they were packing up some works of art in the Tate Gallery in London. And I thought…"

"Boil Some Water – Lots of It"

P AT HOBBY SAT IN HIS OFFICE in the writers' building and looked at his morning's work, just come back from the script department. He was on a "polish job", about the only kind he ever got nowadays. He was to repair a messy sequence in a hurry, but the word "hurry" neither frightened nor inspired him, for Pat had been in Hollywood since he was thirty – now he was forty-nine. All the work he had done this morning (except a little changing around of lines so he could claim them as his own), all he had actually invented, was a single imperative sentence, spoken by a doctor.

"Boil some water – lots of it."

It was a good line. It had sprung into his mind full-grown as soon as he had read the script. In the old silent days Pat would have used it as a spoken title and ended his dialogue worries for a space, but he needed some spoken words for other people in the scene. Nothing came.

"Boil some water," he repeated to himself. "Lot's of it."

The word "boil" brought a quick glad thought of the commissary. A reverent thought too – for an old-timer like Pat, what people you sat with at lunch was more important in getting along than what you dictated in your office. This was no art, as he often said – this was an industry.

"This is no art," he remarked to Max Leam, who was leisurely drinking at a corridor water cooler. "This is an industry."

Max had flung him this timely bone of three weeks at three fifty.

"Say look, Pat! Have you got anything down on paper yet?"

"Say I've got some stuff already that'll make 'em..." He named a familiar biological function with the somewhat startling assurance that it would take place in the theatre.

Max tried to gauge his sincerity.

"Want to read it to me now?" he asked.

"Not yet. But it's got the old guts if you know what I mean."

Max was full of doubts.

"Well, go to it. And if you run into any medical snags check with the doctor over at the First Aid Station. It's got to be right."

The spirit of Pasteur shone firmly in Pat's eyes.

"It will be."

He felt good walking across the lot with Max – so good that he decided to glue himself to the producer and sit down with him at the Big Table. But Max foiled his intention by cooing "See you later" and slipping into the barber shop.

Once Pat had been a familiar figure at the Big Table; often in his golden prime he had dined in the private canteens of executives. Being of the older Hollywood, he understood their jokes, their vanities, their social system with its swift fluctuations. But there were too many new faces at the Big Table now – faces that looked at him with the universal Hollywood suspicion. And at the little tables where the young writers sat they seemed to take work so seriously. As for just sitting down anywhere, even with secretaries or extras – Pat would rather catch a sandwich at the corner.

Detouring to the Red Cross Station, he asked for the doctor. A girl, a nurse, answered from a wall mirror, where she was hastily drawing her lips, "He's out. What is it?"

"Oh. Then I'll come back."

She had finished, and now she turned – vivid and young and with a bright consoling smile.

"Miss Stacey will help you. I'm about to go to lunch."

He was aware of an old, old feeling – left over from the time when he had had wives – a feeling that to invite this little beauty to lunch might cause trouble. But he remembered quickly that he didn't have any wives now – they had both given up asking for alimony.

"I'm working on a medical," he said. "I need some help."

"A medical?"

"Writing it – idea about a doc. Listen – let me buy you lunch. I want to ask you some medical questions."

The nurse hesitated.

"I don't know. It's my first day out here."

"It's all right," he assured her. "Studios are democratic: everybody is just 'Joe' or 'Mary' – from the big shots right down to the prop boys."

He proved it magnificently on their way to lunch by greeting a male star and getting his own name back in return. And in the commissary, where they were placed hard by the Big Table, his producer, Max Leam, looked up, did a little "takem" and winked.

The nurse — her name was Helen Earle — peered about eagerly.

"I don't see anybody," she said. "Except, oh, there's Ronald Colman.* I didn't know Ronald Colman looked like that."

Pat pointed suddenly to the floor.

"And there's Mickey Mouse!"

She jumped and Pat laughed at his joke — but Helen Earle was already staring starry-eyed at the costume extras who filled the hall with the colours of the First Empire. Pat was piqued to see her interest go out to these nonentities.

"The big shots are at this next table," he said solemnly, wistfully, "directors and all except the biggest executives. They could have Ronald Colman pressing pants. I usually sit over there, but they don't want ladies. At lunch, that is, they don't want ladies."

"Oh," said Helen Earle, polite but unimpressed. "It must be wonderful to be a writer too. It's so very interesting."

"It has its points," he said... he had thought for years it was a dog's life.

"What is it you want to ask me about a doctor?"

Here was toil again. Something in Pat's mind snapped off when he thought of the story.

"Well, Max Leam — that man facing us — Max Leam and I have a script about a doc. You know? Like a hospital picture?"

"I know." And she added after a moment, "That's the reason that I went in training."

"And we've got to have it *right*, because a hundred million people would check on it. So this doctor in the script he tells them to boil some water. He says, 'Boil some water – lots of it.' And we were wondering what the people would do then."

"Why – they'd probably boil it," Helen said, and then, somewhat confused by the question, "What people?"

"Well, somebody's daughter and the man that lived there and an attorney and the man that was hurt."

Helen tried to digest this before answering.

"…and some other guy I'm going to cut out," he finished.

There was a pause. The waitress set down tuna-fish sandwiches.

"Well, when a doctor gives orders they're orders," Helen decided.

"Hm." Pat's interest had wandered to an odd little scene at the Big Table while he enquired absently, "You married?"

"No."

"Neither am I."

Beside the Big Table stood an extra. A Russian Cossack with a fierce moustache. He stood resting his hand on the back of an empty chair between Director Paterson and Producer Leam.

"Is this taken?" he asked, with a thick Central European accent.

All along the Big Table faces stared suddenly at him. Until after the first look the supposition was that he must be some well-known actor. But he was not – he was dressed in one of the many-coloured uniforms that dotted the room.

Someone at the table said: "That's taken." But the man drew out the chair and sat down.

"Got to eat somewhere," he remarked with a grin.

A shiver went over the nearby tables. Pat Hobby stared with his mouth ajar. It was as if someone had crayoned Donald Duck into the *Last Supper*.

"Look at that," he advised Helen. "What they'll do to him! Boy!"

The flabbergasted silence at the Big Table was broken by Ned Harman, the production manager.

"This table is reserved," he said.

The extra looked up from a menu.

"They told me sit anywhere."

He beckoned a waitress — who hesitated, looking for an answer in the faces of her superiors.

"Extras don't eat here," said Max Leam, still politely.

"This is a—"

"I got to eat," said the Cossack doggedly. "I been standing around six hours while they shoot this stinking mess and now I got to eat."

The silence had extended — from Pat's angle all within range seemed to be poised in mid-air.

The extra shook his head wearily.

"I dunno who cooked it up..." he said — and Max Leam sat forward in his chair — "but it's the lousiest tripe I ever seen shot in Hollywood."

At his table Pat was thinking why didn't they do something? Knock him down, drag him away. If they were yellow themselves they could call the studio police.

"Who is that?" Helen Earle was following his eyes innocently. "Somebody I ought to know?"

He was listening attentively to Max Leam's voice, raised in anger.

"Get up and get out of here, buddy, and get out quick!"

The extra frowned.

"Who's telling me?" he demanded.

"You'll see." Max appealed to the table at large: "Where's Cushman – where's the Personnel man?"

"You try to move me," said the extra, lifting the hilt of his scabbard above the level of the table, "and I'll hang this on your ear. I know my rights."

The dozen men at the table, representing a thousand dollars an hour in salaries, sat stunned. Far down by the door one of the studio police caught wind of what was happening and started to elbow through the crowded room. And Big Jack Wilson, another director, was on his feet in an instant coming around the table.

But they were too late – Pat Hobby could stand no more. He had jumped up, seizing a big heavy tray from the serving stand nearby. In two springs he reached the scene of action – lifting the tray he brought it down upon the extra's head with all the strength of his forty-nine years. The extra, who had been in the act of rising to meet Wilson's threatened assault, got the blow full on his face and temple, and as he collapsed a dozen red streaks sprang into sight through the heavy grease paint. He crashed sideways between the chairs.

Pat stood over him panting – the tray in his hand.

"The dirty rat!" he cried. "Where does he think——"

The studio policeman pushed past; Wilson pushed past – the two aghast men from another table rushed up to survey the situation.

"It was a gag!" one of them shouted. "That's Walter Herrick, the writer. It's his picture."

"My God!"

"He was kidding Max Leam. It was a gag I tell you!"

"Pull him out... Get a doctor... Look out, there!"

Now Helen Earle hurried over; Walter Herrick was dragged out into a cleared space on the floor and there were yells of "Who did it? Who beaned him?"

Pat let the tray lapse to a chair, its sound unnoticed in the confusion.

He saw Helen Earle working swiftly at the man's head with a pile of clean napkins.

"Why did they have to do this to him?" someone shouted.

Pat caught Max Leam's eye, but Max happened to look away at the moment and a sense of injustice came over Pat. He alone in this crisis, real or imaginary, had *acted*. He alone had played the man, while those stuffed shirts let themselves be insulted and abused. And now he would have to take the rap – because Walter Herrick was powerful and popular, a three-thousand-a-week man who wrote hit shows in New York. How could anyone have guessed that it was a gag?

There was a doctor now. Pat saw him say something to the manageress and her shrill voice sent the waitresses scattering like leaves towards the kitchen.

"Boil some water! Lots of it!"

The words fell wild and unreal on Pat's burdened soul. But even though he now knew at first hand what came next, he did not think that he could go on from there.

Teamed with Genius

1

"I TOOK A CHANCE in sending for you," said Jack Berners. "But there's a job that you just *may* be able to help out with."

Though Pat Hobby was not offended, either as man or writer, a formal protest was called for.

"I been in the industry fifteen years, Jack. I've got more screen credits than a dog has got fleas."

"Maybe I chose the wrong word," said Jack. "What I mean is: that was a long time ago. About money, we'll pay you just what Republic paid you last month – three fifty a week. Now – did you ever hear of a writer named René Wilcox?"

The name was unfamiliar. Pat had scarcely opened a book in a decade.

"She's pretty good," he ventured.

"It's a man, an English playwright. He's only here in LA for his health. Well – we've had a Russian Ballet picture kicking around for a year – three bad scripts on it. So last week we signed up René Wilcox – he seemed just the person."

Pat considered.

"You mean he's—"

"I don't know and I don't care," interrupted Berners sharply. "We think we can borrow Zorina, so we want to hurry things up – do a shooting script instead of just a treatment. Wilcox is inexperienced and that's where you come in. You used to be a good man for structure."

"*Used* to be!"

"All right, maybe you still are." Jack beamed with momentary encouragement, "Find yourself an office and get together with René Wilcox." As Pat started out he called him back and put a bill in his hand. "First of all, get a new hat. You used to be quite a boy around the secretaries in the old days. Don't give up at forty-nine!"

Over in the Writers' Building, Pat glanced at the directory in the hall and knocked at the door of 216. No answer, but he went in to discover a blond, willowy youth of twenty-five staring moodily out the window.

"Hello, René!" Pat said. "I'm your partner."

Wilcox's regard questioned even his existence, but Pat continued heartily. "I hear we're going to lick some stuff into shape. Ever collaborate before?"

"I have never written for the cinema before."

While this increased Pat's chance for a screen credit he badly needed, it meant that he might have to do some work. The very thought made him thirsty.

"This is different from play-writing," he suggested, with suitable gravity.

"Yes – I read a book about it."

Pat wanted to laugh. In 1928 he and another man had concocted such a sucker trap, *Secrets of Film Writing*. It would have made money if pictures hadn't started to talk.

"It all seems simple enough," said Wilcox. Suddenly he took his hat from the rack. "I'll be running along now."

"Don't you want to talk about the script?" demanded Pat. "What have you done so far?"

"I've not done anything," said Wilcox deliberately. "That idiot, Berners, gave me some trash and told me to go on from there. But it's too dismal." His blue eyes narrowed. "I say, what's a boom shot?"

"A boom shot? Why, that's when the camera's on a crane."

Pat leant over the desk and picked up a blue-jacketed *Treatment*. On the cover he read:

BALLET SHOES

A Treatment

by

Consuela Martin

An Original from an idea by Consuela Martin

Pat glanced at the beginning and then at the end.

"I'd like it better if we could get the war in somewhere," he said frowning. "Have the dancer go as a Red Cross nurse and then she could get regenerated. See what I mean?"

There was no answer. Pat turned and saw the door softly closing.

What is this? he exclaimed. What kind of collaborating can a man do if he walks out? Wilcox had not even given the legitimate excuse – the races at Santa Anita!

The door opened again, a pretty girl's face, rather frightened, showed itself momentarily, said "Oh" and disappeared. Then it returned.

"Why it's Mr Hobby!" she exclaimed. "I was looking for Mr Wilcox."

He fumbled for her name but she supplied it.

"Katherine Hodge. I was your secretary when I worked here three years ago."

Pat knew she had once worked with him, but for the moment could not remember whether there had been a deeper relation. It did not seem to him that it had been love – but, looking at her now, that appeared rather too bad.

"Sit down," said Pat. "You assigned to Wilcox?"

"I thought so – but he hasn't given me any work yet."

"I think he's nuts," Pat said gloomily. "He asked me what a boom shot was. Maybe he's sick – that's why he's out here. He'll probably start throwing up all over the office."

"He's well now," Katherine ventured.

"He doesn't look like it to me. Come on in my office. You can work for *me* this afternoon."

Pat lay on his couch while Miss Katherine Hodge read the script of *Ballet Shoes* aloud to him. About midway in the second sequence he fell asleep with his new hat on his chest.

2

Except for the hat, that was the identical position in which he found René next day at eleven. And it was that way for three straight days – one was asleep or else the other – and sometimes both. On the fourth day they had several conferences in which Pat again put forward his idea about the war as a regenerating force for ballet dancers.

"Couldn't we *not* talk about the war?" suggested René. "I have two brothers in the Guards."

"You're lucky to be here in Hollywood."

"That's as it may be."

"Well, what's your idea of the start of the picture?"

"I do not like the present beginning. It gives me an almost physical nausea."

"So then, we got to have something in its place. That's why I want to plant the war—"

"I'm late to luncheon," said René Wilcox. "Goodbye, Mike."

Pat grumbled to Katherine Hodge:

"He can call me anything he likes, but somebody's got to write this picture. I'd go to Jack Berners and tell him – but I think we'd both be out on our ears."

For two days more he camped in René's office, trying to rouse him to action, but with no avail. Desperate on the following day – when the playwright did not even come to the studio – Pat took a Benzedrine tablet and attacked the story alone. Pacing his office with the treatment in his hand he dictated to

Katherine — interspersing the dictation with a short, biased history of his life in Hollywood. At the day's end he had two pages of script.

The ensuing week was the toughest in his life — not even a moment to make a pass at Katherine Hodge. Gradually, with many creaks, his battered hulk got in motion. Benzedrine and great drafts of coffee woke him in the morning, whiskey anaesthetized him at night. Into his feet crept an old neuritis and as his nerves began to crackle he developed a hatred against René Wilcox, which served him as a sort of ersatz fuel. He was going to finish the script by himself and hand it to Berners with the statement that Wilcox had not contributed a single line.

But it was too much — Pat was too far gone. He blew up when he was half through and went on a twenty-four-hour bat — and next morning arrived back at the studio to find a message that Mr Berners wanted to see the script at four. Pat was in a sick and confused state when his door opened and René Wilcox came in with a typescript in one hand and a copy of Berners's note in the other.

"It's all right," said Wilcox. "I've finished it."

"*What?* Have you been *working?*"

"I always work at night."

"What've you done? A treatment?"

"No, a shooting script. At first I was held back by personal worries, but once I got started it was very simple. You just get behind the camera and dream."

Pat stood up aghast.

"But we were supposed to collaborate. Jack'll be wild."

"I've always worked alone," said Wilcox gently. "I'll explain to Berners this afternoon."

Pat sat in a daze. If Wilcox's script was good – but how could a first script be good? – Wilcox should have fed it to him as he wrote; then they might have *had* something.

Fear started his mind working – he was struck by his first original idea since he had been on the job. He phoned to the script department for Katherine Hodge and when she came over told her what he wanted. Katherine hesitated.

"I just want to *read* it," Pat said hastily. "If Wilcox is there you can't take it, of course. But he just might be out."

He waited nervously. In five minutes she was back with the script.

"It isn't mimeographed or even bound," she said.

He was at the typewriter, trembling as he picked out a letter with two fingers.

"Can I help?" she asked.

"Find me a plain envelope and a used stamp and some paste."

Pat sealed the letter himself and then gave directions:

"Listen outside Wilcox's office. If he's in, push it under his door. If he's out get a call boy to deliver it to him, wherever he is. Say it's from the mail room. Then you better go off the lot for the afternoon. So he won't catch on, see?"

As she went out, Pat wished he had kept a copy of the note. He was proud of it – there was a ring of factual sincerity in it too often missing from his work.

Dear Mr Wilcox:

I am sorry to tell you your two brothers were killed in action today by a long-range tommy gun. You are wanted at home in England right away.

John Smythe

The British Consulate, New York

But Pat realized that this was no time for self-applause.

He opened Wilcox's script.

To his vast surprise it was technically proficient – the dissolves, fades, cuts, pans and trucking shots were correctly detailed. This simplified everything. Turning back to the first page he wrote at the top:

BALLET SHOES

First Revise

From Pat Hobby and René Wilcox – presently changing this to read: From René Wilcox and Pat Hobby.

Then, working frantically, he made several dozen small changes. He substituted the word "Scram!" for "Get out of my sight!", he put "Behind the eight ball" instead of "In trouble", and replaced "You'll be sorry" with the apt coinage "Or else!" Then he phoned the script department.

"This is Pat Hobby. I've been working on a script with René Wilcox, and Mr Berners would like to have it mimeographed by half-past three."

This would give him an hour's start on his unconscious collaborator.

"Is it an emergency?"

"I'll say."

"We'll have to split it up between several girls."

Pat continued to improve the script till the call boy arrived. He wanted to put in his war idea, but time was short – still, he finally told the call boy to sit down, while he wrote laboriously in pencil on the last page.

CLOSE SHOT: *Boris and Rita*

Rita: *What does anything matter now! I have enlisted as a trained nurse in the war.*

Boris (moved): War purifies and regenerates!

(He puts his arms around her in a wild embrace as the music soars way up and we FADE OUT)

Limp and exhausted by his effort he needed a drink, so he left the lot and slipped cautiously into the bar across from the studio, where he ordered gin and water.

With the glow, he thought warm thoughts. He had done *almost* what he had been hired to do – though his hand had accidentally fallen upon the dialogue rather than the structure. But how could Berners tell that the structure wasn't Pat's? Katherine Hodge would say nothing, for fear of implicating herself. They were all guilty, but guiltiest of all was René Wilcox for refusing to play the game. Always, according to his lights, Pat had played the game.

He had another drink, bought breath tablets and for a while amused himself at the nickel machine in the drugstore. Louie, the studio bookie, asked if he was interested in wagers on a bigger scale.

"Not today, Louie."

"What are they paying you, Pat?"

"Thousand a week."

"Not so bad."

"Oh, a lot of us old-timers are coming back," Pat prophesied. "In silent days was where you got real training – with directors shooting off the cuff and needing a gag in a split second. Now it's a sis job. They got English teachers working in pictures! What do they know?"

"How about a little something on Quaker Girl?"

"No," said Pat. "This afternoon I got an important angle to work on. I don't want to worry about horses."

At three fifteen he returned to his office to find two copies of his script in bright new covers.

BALLET SHOES
from
René Wilcox and Pat Hobby
First Revise

It reassured him to see his name in type. As he waited in Jack Berners's ante-room he almost wished he had reversed the names. With the right director this might be another *It Happened One*

Night, and if he got his name on something like that it meant a three- or four-year gravy ride. But this time he'd save his money – go to Santa Anita only once a week – get himself a girl along the type of Katherine Hodge, who wouldn't expect a mansion in Beverly Hills.

Berners's secretary interrupted his reverie, telling him to go in. As he entered, he saw with gratification that a copy of the new script lay on Berners's desk.

"Did you ever," asked Berners suddenly, "go to a psychoanalyst?"

"No," admitted Pat. "But I suppose I could get up on it. Is it a new assignment?"

"Not exactly. It's just that I think you've lost your grip. Even larceny requires a certain cunning. I've just talked to Wilcox on the phone."

"Wilcox must be nuts," said Pat aggressively. "I didn't steal anything from him. His name's on it, isn't it? Two weeks ago I laid out all his structure – every scene. I even wrote one whole scene – at the end about the war."

"Oh yes, the war," said Berners, as if he was thinking of something else.

"But if you like Wilcox's ending better—"

"Yes, I like his ending better. I never saw a man pick up this work so fast." He paused. "Pat, you've told the truth just once since you came in this room – that you didn't steal anything from Wilcox."

"I certainly did not. I *gave* him stuff."

But a certain dreariness, a grey malaise, crept over him as Berners continued:

"I told you we had three scripts. You used an old one we discarded a year ago. Wilcox was in when your secretary arrived, and he sent one of them to you. Clever, eh?"

Pat was speechless.

"You see, he and that girl like each other. Seems she typed a play for him this summer."

"They like each other," said Pat incredulously. "Why, he—"

"Hold it, Pat. You've had trouble enough today."

"He's responsible," Pat cried. "He wouldn't collaborate – and all the time…"

"…he was writing a swell script. And he can write his own ticket if we can persuade him to stay here and do another."

Pat could stand no more. He stood up.

"Anyhow, thank you, Jack," he faltered. "Call my agent if anything turns up." Then he bolted suddenly and surprisingly for the door.

Jack Berners signalled on the Dictograph for the President's office.

"Get a chance to read it?" he asked in a tone of eagerness.

"It's swell. Better than you said. Wilcox is with me now."

"Have you signed him up?"

"I'm going to. Seems he wants to work with Hobby. Here, you talk to him."

Wilcox's rather high voice came over the wire.

"Must have Mike Hobby," he said. "Grateful to him. Had a quarrel with a certain young lady just before he came, but today Hobby brought us together. Besides, I want to write a

43

play about him. So give him to me – you fellows don't want him any more."

Berners picked up his secretary's phone.

"Go after Pat Hobby. He's probably in the bar across the street. We're putting him on salary again, but we'll be sorry."

He switched off, switched on again.

"Oh! Take him his hat. He forgot his hat."

Pat Hobby and Orson Welles

1

"WHO'S THIS WELLES?" Pat asked of Louie, the studio bookie. "Every time I pick up a paper they got about this Welles."

"You know, he's that beard," explained Louie.

"Sure, I know he's that beard, you couldn't miss that. But what credits's he got? What's he done to draw one hundred and fifty grand a picture?"

What indeed? Had he, like Pat, been in Hollywood over twenty years? Did he have credits that would knock your eye out, extending up to... well, up to five years ago, when Pat's credits had begun to be few and far between?

"Listen – they don't last long," said Louie consolingly. "We've seen 'em come and we've seen 'em go. Hey, Pat?"

Yes – but meanwhile those who had toiled in the vineyard through the heat of the day were lucky to get a few weeks at three fifty. Men who had once had wives and Filipinos and swimming pools.

"Maybe it's the beard," said Louie. "Maybe you and I should grow a beard. My father had a beard, but it never got him off Grand Street."

The gift of hope had remained with Pat through his misfortunes – and the valuable alloy of his hope was proximity. Above all things one must stick around, one must be there when the glazed, tired mind of the producer grappled with the question "Who?" So presently Pat wandered out of the drugstore and crossed the street to the lot that was home.

As he passed through the side entrance an unfamiliar studio policeman stood in his way.

"Everybody in the front entrance now."

"I'm Hobby, the writer," Pat said.

The Cossack was unimpressed.

"Got your card?"

"I'm between pictures. But I've got an engagement with Jack Berners."

"Front gate."

As he turned away, Pat thought savagely: "Lousy Keystone Cop!" In his mind he shot it out with him. Plunk! The stomach. Plunk! Plunk! Plunk!

At the main entrance, too, there was a new face.

"Where's Ike?" Pat demanded.

"Ike's gone."

"Well, it's all right, I'm Pat Hobby. Ike always passes me."

"That's why he's gone," said the guardian blandly. "Who's your business with?"

Pat hesitated. He hated to disturb a producer.

"Call Jack Berners's office," he said. "Just speak to his secretary."

After a minute the man turned from the phone.

"What about?" he said.

"About a picture."

He waited for an answer.

"She wants to know what picture?"

"To hell with it," said Pat disgustedly. "Look – call Louie Griebel. What's all this about?"

"Orders from Mr Kasper," said the clerk. "Last week a visitor from Chicago fell in the wind machine – hello. Mr Louie Griebel?"

"I'll talk to him," said Pat, taking the phone.

"I can't do nothing, Pat," mourned Louie. "I had trouble getting my boy in this morning. Some twerp from Chicago fell in the wind machine."

"What's that got to do with me?" demanded Pat vehemently.

He walked, a little faster than his wont, along the studio wall to the point where it joined the back lot. There was a guard there, but there were always people passing to and fro and he joined one of the groups. Once inside he would see Jack and have himself excepted from this absurd ban. Why, he had known this lot when the first shacks were rising on it, when this was considered the edge of the desert.

"Sorry, mister, you with this party?"

"I'm in a hurry," said Pat. "I've lost my card."

"Yeah? Well, for all I know you may be a plain-clothes man." He held open a copy of a photo magazine under Pat's nose. "I wouldn't let you in even if you told me you was this here Orson Welles."

2

THERE IS AN OLD CHAPLIN PICTURE about a crowded streetcar where the entrance of one man at the rear forces another out in front. A similar image came into Pat's mind in the ensuing days whenever he thought of Orson Welles. Welles was in; Hobby was out. Never before had the studio been barred to Pat, and though Welles was on another lot it seemed as if his large body, pushing in brashly from nowhere, had edged Pat out the gate.

"Now where do you go?" Pat thought. He had worked in the other studios, but they were not his. At this studio he never felt unemployed – in recent times of stress he had eaten property food on its stages – half a cold lobster during a scene from *The Divine Miss Carstairs*; he had often slept on the sets and last winter made use of a Chesterfield overcoat from the costume department. Orson Welles had no business edging him out of this. Orson Welles belonged with the rest of the snobs back in New York.

On the third day he was frantic with gloom. He had sent note after note to Jack Berners and even asked Louie to intercede – now word came that Jack had left town. There were so few friends left. Desolate, he stood in front of the automobile gate with a crowd of staring children, feeling that he had reached the end at last.

A great limousine rolled out, in the back of which Pat recognized the great overstuffed Roman face of Harold Marcus. The car rolled towards the children and, as one of them ran in front of it, slowed down. The old man spoke into the tube and the car halted. He leant out, blinking.

"Is there no policeman here?" he asked of Pat.

"No, Mr Marcus," said Pat quickly. "There should be. I'm Pat Hobby, the writer – could you give me a lift down the street?"

It was unprecedented – it was an act of desperation, but Pat's need was great.

Mr Marcus looked at him closely.

"Oh yes, I remember you," he said. "Get in."

He might possibly have meant get up in front with the chauffeur. Pat compromised by opening one of the little seats. Mr Marcus was one of the most powerful men in the whole picture world. He did not occupy himself with production any longer. He spent most of his time rocking from coast to coast on fast trains, merging and launching, launching and merging, like a much divorced woman.

"Some day those children'll get hurt."

"Yes, Mr Marcus," agreed Pat heartily. "Mr Marcus—"

"They ought to have a policeman there."

"Yes, Mr Marcus. Mr Marcus—"

"Hm-m-m!" said Mr Marcus. "Where do you want to be dropped?"

Pat geared himself to work fast.

"Mr Marcus, when I was your press agent—"

"I know," said Mr Marcus. "You wanted a ten-dollar-a-week raise."

"What a memory!" cried Pat in gladness. "What a memory! But Mr Marcus, now I don't want anything at all."

"This is a miracle."

"I've got modest wants, see, and I've saved enough to retire."

He thrust his shoes slightly forward under a hanging blanket. The Chesterfield coat effectively concealed the rest.

"That's what I'd like," said Mr Marcus gloomily. "A farm – with chickens. Maybe a little nine-hole course. Not even a stock ticker."

"I want to retire, but different," said Pat earnestly. "Pictures have been my life. I want to watch them grow and grow—"

Mr Marcus groaned.

"Till they explode," he said. "Look at Fox! I cried for him." He pointed to his eyes. "Tears!"

Pat nodded very sympathetically.

"I want only one thing." From the long familiarity he went into the foreign locution. "I should go on the lot any time. From nothing. Only to be there. Should bother nobody. Only help a little from nothing if any young person wants advice."

"See Berners," said Marcus.

"He said see you."

"Then you did want something." Marcus smiled. "All right, all right by me. Where do you get off now?"

"Could you write me a pass?" Pat pleaded. "Just a word on your card?"

"I'll look into it," said Mr Marcus. "Just now I've got things on my mind. I'm going to a luncheon." He sighed profoundly. "They want I should meet this new Orson Welles that's in Hollywood."

Pat's heart winced. There it was again – that name, sinister and remorseless, spreading like a dark cloud over all his skies.

"Mr Marcus," he said so sincerely that his voice trembled, "I wouldn't be surprised if Orson Welles is the biggest menace that's come to Hollywood for years. He gets a hundred and fifty grand a picture and I wouldn't be surprised if he was so radical that you had to have all-new equipment and start all over again like you did with sound in 1928."

"Oh my God!" groaned Mr Marcus.

"And me," said Pat, "all I want is a pass and no money – to leave things as they are."

Mr Marcus reached for his card case.

3

To those grouped together under the name "talent", the atmosphere of a studio is not unfailingly bright – one fluctuates too quickly between high hope and grave apprehension. Those few who decide things are happy in their work and sure that they are worthy of their hire – the rest live in a mist of doubt as to when their vast inadequacy will be disclosed.

Pat's psychology was, oddly, that of the masters, and for the most part he was unworried, even though he was off salary. But there was one large fly in the ointment – for the first time in his life he began to feel a loss of identity. Due to reasons that he did not quite understand, though it might have been traced to his conversation, a number of people began to address him as "Orson".

Now to lose one's identity is a careless thing in any case. But to lose it to an enemy, or at least to one who has become scapegoat for our misfortunes – that is a hardship. Pat was *not* Orson. Any resemblance must be faint and far-fetched and he was aware of the fact. The final effect was to make him, in that regard, something of an eccentric.

"Pat," said Joe the barber, "Orson was in here today and asked me to trim his beard."

"I hope you set fire to it," said Pat.

"I did," Joe winked at waiting customers over a hot towel. "He asked for a singe, so I took it all off. Now his face is as bald as yours. In fact you look a bit alike."

This was the morning the kidding was so ubiquitous that, to avoid it, Pat lingered in Mario's bar across the street. He was not drinking – at the bar, that is, for he was down to his last thirty cents, but he refreshed himself frequently from a half-pint in his back pocket. He needed the stimulus, for he had to make a touch presently and he knew that money was easier to borrow when one didn't have an air of urgent need.

His quarry, Jeff Boldini, was in an unsympathetic state of mind. He too was an artist, albeit a successful one, and a certain great lady of the screen had just burnt him up by criticizing a wig he had made for her. He told the story to Pat at length and the latter waited until it was all out before broaching his request.

"No soap," said Jeff. "Hell, you never paid me back what you borrowed last month."

"But I got a job now," lied Pat. "This is just to tide me over. I start tomorrow."

"If they don't give the job to Orson Welles," said Jeff humorously.

Pat's eyes narrowed but he managed to utter a polite, borrower's laugh.

"Hold it," said Jeff. "You know I think you look like him?"

"Yeah."

"Honest. Anyhow I could make you look like him. I could make you a beard that would be his double."

"I wouldn't be his double for fifty grand."

With his head on one side Jeff regarded Pat.

"I could," he said. "Come on into my chair and let me see."

"Like hell."

"Come on. I'd like to try it. You haven't got anything to do. You don't work till tomorrow."

"I don't want a beard."

"It'll come off."

"I don't want it."

"It won't cost you anything. In fact I'll be paying *you* – I'll loan you the ten smackers if you'll let me make you a beard."

Half an hour later Jeff looked at his completed work.

"It's perfect," he said. "Not only the beard, but the eyes and everything."

"All right. Now take it off," said Pat moodily.

"What's the hurry? That's a fine muff. That's a work of art. We ought to put a camera on it. Too bad you're working tomorrow – they're using a dozen beards out on Sam Jones's set and one of them went to jail in a homo raid. I bet with that muff you could get the job."

It was weeks since Pat had heard the word "job" and he could not himself say how he managed to exist and eat. Jeff saw the light in his eye.

"What say? Let me drive you out there just for fun," pleaded Jeff. "I'd like to see if Sam could tell it was a phoney muff."

"I'm a writer, not a ham."

"Come on! Nobody would never know you back of that. And you'd draw another ten bucks."

As they left the make-up department Jeff lingered behind a minute. On a strip of cardboard he crayoned the name Orson Welles in large block letters. And outside, without Pat's notice, he stuck it in the windshield of his car.

He did not go directly to the back lot. Instead he drove not too swiftly up the main studio street. In front of the administration building he stopped on the pretext that the engine was missing, and almost in no time a small but definitely interested crowd began to gather. But Jeff's plans did not include stopping anywhere long, so he hopped in and they started on a tour around the commissary.

"Where are we going?" demanded Pat.

He had already made one nervous attempt to tear the beard from him, but to his surprise it did not come away.

He complained of this to Jeff.

"Sure," Jeff explained. "That's made to last. You'll have to soak it off."

The car paused momentarily at the door of the commissary. Pat saw blank eyes staring at him and he stared back at them blankly from the rear seat.

"You'd think I was the only beard on the lot," he said gloomily.

"You can sympathize with Orson Welles."

"To hell with him."

This colloquy would have puzzled those without, to whom he was nothing less than the real McCoy.

Jeff drove on slowly up the street. Ahead of them a little group of men were walking – one of them, turning, saw the car and drew the attention of the others to it. Whereupon the most elderly member of the party threw up his arms in what appeared to be a defensive gesture, and plunged to the sidewalk as the car went past.

"My God, did you see that?" exclaimed Jeff. "That was Mr Marcus."

He came to a stop. An excited man ran up and put his head in the car window.

"Mr Welles, our Mr Marcus has had a heart attack. Can we use your car to get him to the infirmary?"

Pat stared. Then very quickly he opened the door on the other side and dashed from the car. Not even the beard could impede his streamlined flight. The policeman at the gate, not recognizing the incarnation, tried to have words with him, but Pat shook him off with the ease of a triple-threat back and never paused till he reached Mario's bar.

Three extras with beards stood at the rail, and with relief Pat merged himself into their corporate whiskers. With a trembling hand he took the hard-earned ten-dollar bill from his pocket.

"Set 'em up," he cried hoarsely. "Every muff has a drink on me."

Pat Hobby's Secret

1

DISTRESS IN HOLLYWOOD is endemic and always acute. Scarcely an executive but is being gnawed at by some insoluble problem and in a democratic way he will let you in on it, with no charge. The problem, be it one of health or of production, is faced courageously and with groans at from one to five thousand a week. That's how pictures are made.

"But this one has got me down," said Mr Banizon, "because how did the artillery shell get in the trunk of Claudette Colbert or Betty Field* or whoever we decide to use? We got to explain it so the audience will believe it."

He was in the office of Louie the studio bookie, and his present audience also included Pat Hobby, venerable script stooge of forty-nine. Mr Banizon did not expect a suggestion from either of them, but he had been talking aloud to himself about the problem for a week now and was unable to stop.

"Who's your writer on it?" asked Louie.

"R. Parke Woll," said Banizon indignantly. "First I buy this opening from another writer, see. A grand notion but only a notion. Then I call in R. Parke Woll, the playwright, and we meet a couple of times and develop it. Then when we get the end in sight, his agent horns in and says he won't let Woll talk any more unless I give him a contract – eight weeks at $3,000! And all I need him for is one more day!"

The sum brought a glitter into Pat's old eyes. Ten years ago he had camped beatifically in range of such a salary – now he was lucky to get a few weeks at $250. His inflamed and burnt-over talent had failed to produce a second growth.

"The worse part of it is that Woll told me the ending," continued the producer.

"Then what are you waiting for?" demanded Pat. "You don't need to pay him a cent."

"I forgot it!" groaned Mr Banizon. "Two phones were ringing at once in my office – one from a working director. And while I was talking Woll had to run along. Now I can't remember it and I can't get him back."

Perversely Pat Hobby's sense of justice was with the producer, not the writer. Banizon had almost outsmarted Woll and then been cheated by a tough break. And now the playwright, with the insolence of an Eastern snob, was holding him up for twenty-four grand. What with the European market gone. What with the war.

"Now he's on a big bat," said Banizon. "I know because I got a man tailing him. It's enough to drive you nuts – here I got the whole story except the pay-off. What good is it to me like that?"

"If he's drunk maybe he'd spill it," suggested Louie practically.

"Not to me," said Mr Banizon. "I thought of it, but he would recognize my face."

Having reached the end of his current blind alley, Mr Banizon picked a horse in the third and one in the seventh and prepared to depart.

"I got an idea," said Pat.

Mr Banizon looked suspiciously at the red old eyes.

"I got no time to hear it now," he said.

"I'm not selling anything," Pat reassured him. "I got a deal almost ready over at Paramount. But once I worked with this R. Parke Woll and maybe I could find what you want to know."

He and Mr Banizon went out of the office together and walked slowly across the lot. An hour later, for an advance consideration of fifty dollars, Pat was employed to discover how a live artillery shell got into Claudette Colbert's trunk or Betty Field's trunk or whosoever's trunk it should be.

2

THE SWATH WHICH R. PARKE WOLL was now cutting through the City of the Angels would have attracted no special notice in the Twenties; in the fearful Forties it rang out like laughter in church. He was easy to follow: his absence had been requested from two hotels, but he had settled down into a routine where he carried his sleeping quarters in his elbow. A small but alert band of rats and weasels were furnishing him moral support in his journey – a journey which Pat caught up with at two a.m. in Conk's Old-Fashioned Bar.

Conk's Bar was haughtier than its name, boasting cigarette girls and a doorman-bouncer named Smith who had once stayed a full hour with Tarzan White. Mr Smith was an embittered man who expressed himself by goosing the patrons on their way in and out, and this was Pat's introduction. When he recovered himself, he discovered R. Parke Woll in a mixed company around a table, and sauntered up with an air of surprise.

"Hello, good-looking," he said to Woll. "Remember me – Pat Hobby?"

R. Parke Woll brought him with difficulty into focus, turning his head first on one side then on the other, letting it sink, snap up and then lash forward like a cobra taking a candid snapshot. Evidently it recorded, for he said:

"Pat Hobby! Sit down and wha'll you have. Gen'lemen, this is Pat Hobby – best left-handed writer in Hollywood. Pat h'are you?"

Pat sat down, amid suspicious looks from a dozen predatory eyes. Was Pat an old friend sent to get the playwright home?

Pat saw this and waited until a half-hour later when he found himself alone with Woll in the washroom.

"Listen, Parke, Banizon is having you followed," he said. "I don't know why he's doing it. Louie at the studio tipped me off."

"You don't know why?" cried Parke. "Well, I know why. I got something he wants – that's why!"

"You owe him money?"

"Owe him money. Why that… he owes *me* money! He owes me for three long, hard conferences – I outlined a whole damn picture for him." His vague finger tapped his forehead in several places. "What he wants is in here."

An hour passed at the turbulent orgiastic table. Pat waited – and then inevitably in the slow, limited cycle of the lush, Woll's mind returned to the subject.

"The funny thing is I told him who put the shell in the trunk and why. And then the mastermind forgot."

Pat had an inspiration.

"But his secretary remembered."

"She did?" Woll was flabbergasted. "Secretary – don't remember secretary."

"She came in," ventured Pat uneasily.

"Well then by God he's got to pay me or I'll sue him."

"Banizon says he's got a better idea."

"The hell he has. My idea was a pip. Listen…"

He spoke for two minutes.

"You like it?" he demanded. He looked at Pat for applause – then he must have seen something in Pat's eye that he was not intended to see. "Why you little skunk," he cried. "You've talked to Banizon – he sent you here."

Pat rose and tore like a rabbit for the door. He would have been out into the street before Woll could overtake him, had it not been for the intervention of Mr Smith, the doorman.

"Where you going?" he demanded, catching Pat by his lapels.

"Hold him!" cried Woll, coming up. He aimed a blow at Pat which missed and landed full in Mr Smith's mouth.

It has been mentioned that Mr Smith was an embittered as well as a powerful man. He dropped Pat, picked up R. Parke Woll by crotch and shoulder, held him high and then in one gigantic pound brought his body down against the floor. Three minutes later Woll was dead.

3

EXCEPT IN GREAT SCANDALS like the Arbuckle case* the industry protects its own – and the industry included Pat, however intermittently. He was let out of prison next morning without bail, wanted only as a material witness. If anything, the publicity was advantageous – for the first time in a year his name appeared in the trade journals. Moreover, he was now the only living man who knew how the shell got into Claudette Colbert's (or Betty Field's) trunk.

"When can you come up and see me?" said Mr Banizon.

"After the inquest tomorrow," said Pat enjoying himself. "I feel kind of shaken – it gave me an earache."

That too indicated power. Only those who were "in" could speak of their health and be listened to.

"Woll really did tell you?" questioned Banizon.

"He told me," said Pat. "And it's worth more than fifty smackers. I'm going to get me a new agent and bring him to your office."

"I tell you a better plan," said Banizon hastily. "I'll get you on the payroll. Four weeks at your regular price."

"What's my price?" demanded Pat gloomily. "I've drawn every-thing from four thousand to zero." And he added ambiguously, "As Shakespeare says, 'Every man has his price.'"

The attendant rodents of R. Parke Woll had vanished with their small plunger into convenient ratholes, leaving as the defendant

Mr Smith, and as witnesses Pat and two frightened cigarette girls. Mr Smith's defence was that he had been attacked. At the inquest, one cigarette girl agreed with him – one condemned him for unnecessary roughness. Pat Hobby's turn was next, but before his name was called he started, as a voice spoke to him from behind.

"You talk against my husband and I'll twist your tongue out by the roots."

A huge dinosaur of a woman, fully six feet tall and broad in proportion, was leaning forward against his chair.

"Pat Hobby, step forward please... now, Mr Hobby, tell us exactly what happened."

The eyes of Mr Smith were fixed balefully on his and he felt the eyes of the bouncer's mate reaching in for his tongue through the back of his head. He was full of natural hesitation.

"I don't know exactly," he said, and then, with quick inspiration, "All I know is everything went white!"

"*What?*"

"That's the way it was. I saw white. Just like some guys see red or black I saw white."

There was some consultation among the authorities.

"Well, what happened from when you came into the restaurant – up to the time you saw white?"

"Well..." said Pat fighting for time. "It was all kind of that way. I came and sat down and then it began to go black."

"You mean white."

"Black *and* white."

There was a general titter.

"Witness dismissed. Defendant remanded for trial."

What was a little joking to endure when the stakes were so high – all that night a mountainous Amazon pursued him through his dreams and he needed a strong drink before appearing at Mr Banizon's office next morning. He was accompanied by one of the few Hollywood agents who had not yet taken him on and shaken him off.

"A flat sum of five hundred," offered Banizon. "Or four weeks at two fifty to work on another picture."

"How bad do you want this?" asked the agent. "My client seems to think it's worth three thousand."

"Of my own money?" cried Banizon. "And it isn't even *his* idea. Now that Woll is dead it's in the Public Remains."

"Not quite," said the agent. "I think like you do that ideas are sort of in the air. They belong to whoever's got them at the time – like balloons."

"Well, how much?" asked Mr Banizon fearfully. "How do I know he's got the idea?"

The agent turned to Pat.

"Shall we let him find out – for a thousand dollars?"

After a moment Pat nodded. Something was bothering him.

"All right," said Banizon. "This strain is driving me nuts. One thousand."

There was silence.

"Spill it Pat," said the agent.

Still no word from Pat. They waited. When Pat spoke at last, his voice seemed to come from afar.

"Everything's white," he gasped.

"*What?*"

"I can't help it – everything has gone white. I can see it – white. I remember going into the joint, but after that it all goes white."

For a moment they thought he was holding out. Then the agent realized that Pat actually had drawn a psychological blank. The secret of R. Parke Woll was safe for ever.

Too late Pat realized that a thousand dollars was slipping away and tried desperately to recover.

"I remember, I remember! It was put in by some Nazi dictator."

"Maybe the girl put it in the trunk herself," said Banizon ironically. "For her bracelet."

For many years Mr Banizon would be somewhat gnawed by this insoluble problem. And as he glowered at Pat he wished that writers could be dispensed with altogether. If only ideas could be plucked from the inexpensive air!

Pat Hobby, Putative Father

1

MOST WRITERS LOOK LIKE WRITERS whether they want to or not. It is hard to say why – for they model their exteriors whimsically on Wall Street brokers, cattle kings or English explorers – but they all turn out looking like writers, as definitely typed as "The Public" or "The Profiteers" in the cartoons.

Pat Hobby was the exception. He did not look like a writer. And only in one corner of the Republic could he have been identified as a member of the entertainment world. Even there the first guess would have been that he was an extra down on his luck, or a bit player who specialized in the sort of father who should *never* come home. But a writer he was: he had collaborated in over two dozen moving-picture scripts, most of them, it must be admitted, prior to 1929.

A writer? He had a desk in the Writers' Building at the studio; he had pencils, paper, a secretary, paper clips, a pad for office memoranda. And he sat in an overstuffed chair, his eyes not so very bloodshot, taking in the morning's *Reporter*.

"I got to get to work," he told Miss Raudenbush at eleven. And again at twelve: "I got to get to work."

At quarter to one, he began to feel hungry – up to this point, every move, or rather every moment, was in the writer's tradition. Even to the faint irritation that no one had annoyed him, no one had bothered him, no one had interfered with the long empty dream which constituted his average day.

He was about to accuse his secretary of staring at him when the welcome interruption came. A studio guide tapped at his door and brought him a note from his boss, Jack Berners:

Dear Pat:
Please take some time off and show these people around the lot.
Jack

"My God!" Pat exclaimed. "How can I be expected to get anything done and show people around the lot at the same time. Who are they?" he demanded of the guide.

"I don't know. One of them seems to be kind of coloured. He looks like the extras they had at Paramount for *Bengal Lancer*. He can't speak English. The other—"

Pat was putting on his coat to see for himself.

"Will you be wanting me this afternoon?" asked Miss Raudenbush.

He looked at her with infinite reproach and went out in front of the Writers' Building.

The visitors were there. The sultry person was tall and of a fine carriage, dressed in excellent English clothes except for a turban. The other was a youth of fifteen, quite light of hue. He also wore a turban with beautifully cut jodhpurs and riding coat.

They bowed formally.

"Hear you want to go on some sets," said Pat. "You friends of Jack Berners?"

"Acquaintances," said the youth. "May I present you to my uncle: Sir Singrim Dak Raj."

Probably, thought Pat, the company was cooking up a *Bengal Lancers*, and this man would play the heavy who owned the Khyber Pass. Maybe they'd put Pat on it – at three fifty a week. Why not? He knew how to write that stuff:

Beautiful Long Shot. The Gorge. Show Tribesman firing from behind rocks.

Medium Shot. Tribesman hit by bullet making nosedive over high rock (use stunt man).

Medium Long Shot. The Valley. British troops wheeling out cannon.

"You going to be long in Hollywood?" he asked shrewdly.

"My uncle doesn't speak English," said the youth in a measured voice. "We are here only a few days. You see – I am your putative son."

2

" AND I WOULD VERY MUCH LIKE to see Bonita Granville,"* continued the youth. "I find she has been borrowed by your studio."

They had been walking towards the production office and it took Pat a minute to grasp what the young man had said.

"You're my what?" he asked.

"Your putative son," said the young man, in a sort of sing-song. "Legally I am the son and heir of the Raja Dak Raj Indore. But I was born John Brown Hobby."

"Yes?" said Pat. "Go on! What's this?"

"My mother was Delia Brown. You married her in 1926. And she divorced you in 1927, when I was a few months old. Later she took me to India, where she married my present legal father."

"Oh," said Pat. They had reached the production office. "You want to see Bonita Granville."

"Yes," said John Hobby Indore. "If it is convenient."

Pat looked at the shooting schedule on the wall.

"It may be," he said heavily. "We can go and see."

As they started towards Stage 4, he exploded.

"What do you mean, 'my potato son'? I'm glad to see you and all that, but say, are you really the kid Delia had in 1926?"

"Putatively," John Indore said. "At that time you and she were legally married."

He turned to his uncle and spoke rapidly in Hindustani, whereupon the latter bent forward, looked with cold examination upon Pat and threw up his shoulders without comment. The whole business was making Pat vaguely uncomfortable.

When he pointed out the commissary, John wanted to stop there "to buy his uncle a hot dog". It seemed that Sir Singrim had conceived a passion for them at the World's Fair in New York, whence they had just come. They were taking ship for Madras tomorrow.

"...whether or not," said John, sombrely, "I get to see Bonita Granville. I do not care if I *meet* her. I am too young for her.

She is already an old woman by our standards. But I'd like to *see* her."

It was one of those bad days for showing people around. Only one of the directors shooting today was an old-timer on whom Pat could count for a welcome – and at the door of that stage he received word that the star kept blowing up in his lines and had demanded that the set be cleared.

In desperation he took his charges out to the back lot and walked them past the false fronts of ships and cities and village streets and medieval gates – a sight in which the boy showed a certain interest, but which Sir Singrim found disappointing. Each time that Pat led them around behind to demonstrate that it was all phoney, Sir Singrim's expression would change to disappointment and faint contempt.

"What's he say?" Pat asked his offspring, after Sir Singrim had walked eagerly into a Fifth Avenue jewellery store, to find nothing but carpenter's rubble inside.

"He is the third richest man in India," said John. "He is disgusted. He says he will never enjoy an American picture again. He says he will buy one of our picture companies in India and make every set as solid as the Taj Mahal. He thinks perhaps the actresses just have a false front too, and that's why you won't let us see them."

The first sentence had rung a sort of carillon in Pat's head. If there was anything he liked it was a good piece of money – not this miserable, uncertain two fifty a week which purchased his freedom.

"I'll tell you," he said with sudden decision. "We'll try Stage 4 and peek at Bonita Granville."

Stage 4 was double-locked and barred for the day – the director hated visitors, and it was a process stage besides. "Process" was a generic name for trick photography in which every studio competed with other studios and lived in terror of spies. More specifically it meant that a projecting machine threw a moving background upon a transparent screen. On the other side of the screen a scene was played and recorded against this moving background. The projector on one side of the screen and the camera on the other were so synchronized that the result could show a star standing on his head before an indifferent crowd on 42nd Street – a *real* crowd and a *real* star – and the poor eye could only conclude that it was being deluded and never quite guess how.

Pat tried to explain this to John, but John was peering for Bonita Granville from behind the great mass of coiled ropes and pails where they hid. They had not got there by the front entrance, but by a little side door for technicians that Pat knew.

Wearied by the long jaunt over the back lot, Pat took a pint flask from his hip and offered it to Sir Singrim, who declined. He did not offer it to John.

"Stunt your growth," he said solemnly, taking a long pull.

"I do not want any," said John with dignity.

He was suddenly alert. He had spotted an idol more glamorous than Shiva not twenty feet away – her back, her profile, her voice. Then she moved off.

Watching his face, Pat was rather touched.

"We can go nearer," he said. "We might get to that ballroom set. They're not using it – they got covers on the furniture."

On tiptoe they started, Pat in the lead, then Sir Singrim, then John. As they moved softly forward, Pat heard the words "Lights" and stopped in his tracks. Then, as a blinding white glow struck at their eyes and the voice shouted "Quiet! We're rolling!" Pat began to run, followed quickly through the white silence by the others.

The silence did not endure.

"*Cut!*" screamed a voice. "What the living, blazing hell!"

From the director's angle something had happened on the screen which, for the moment, was inexplicable. Three gigantic silhouettes, two with huge Indian turbans, had danced across what was intended to be a New England harbour – they had blundered into the line of the process shot. Prince John Indore had not only seen Bonita Granville – he had acted in the same picture. His silhouetted foot seemed to pass miraculously through her blonde young head.

3

THEY SAT FOR SOME TIME in the guardroom before word could be gotten to Jack Berners, who was off the lot. So there was leisure for talk. This consisted of a longish harangue from Sir Singrim to John, which the latter – modifying its tone if not its words – translated to Pat.

"My uncle says his brother wanted to do something for you. He thought perhaps if you were a great writer he might invite you to come to his kingdom and write his life."

"I never claimed to be—"

"My uncle says you are an ignominious writer – in your own land you permitted him to be touched by those dogs of the policemen."

"Aw – bananas," muttered Pat uncomfortably.

"He says my mother always wished you well. But now she is a high and sacred lady and should never see you again. He says we will go to our chambers in the Ambassador Hotel and meditate and pray and let you know what we decide."

When they were released, and the two moguls were escorted apologetically to their car by a studio yes-man, it seemed to Pat that it had been pretty well decided already. He was angry. For the sake of getting his son a peek at Miss Granville, he had quite possibly lost his job – though he didn't really think so. Or rather he was pretty sure that when his week was up he would have lost it anyhow. But though it was a pretty bad break he remembered most clearly from the afternoon that Sir Singrim was "the third richest man in India", and after dinner at a bar on La Cienega he decided to go down to the Ambassador Hotel and find out the result of the prayer and meditation.

It was early dark of a September evening. The Ambassador was full of memories to Pat – the Coconut Grove in the great days, when directors found pretty girls in the afternoon and made stars of them by night. There was some activity in front of the door and Pat watched it idly. Such a quantity of baggage he had seldom seen, even in the train of Gloria Swanson or Joan Crawford.* Then he started as he saw two or three men in turbans moving around among the baggage. So – they were running out on him.

Sir Singrim Dak Raj and his nephew Prince John, both pulling on gloves as if at a command, appeared at the door, as Pat stepped forward out of the darkness.

"Taking a powder, eh?" he said. "Say, when you get back there, tell them that one American could lick—"

"I have left a note for you," said Prince John, turning from his uncle's side. "I say, you were nice this afternoon and it really was too bad."

"Yes, it was," agreed Pat.

"But we are providing for you," John said. "After our prayers we decided that you will receive fifty sovereigns a month – two hundred and fifty dollars – for the rest of your natural life."

"What will I have to do for it?" questioned Pat suspiciously.

"It will only be withdrawn in case…"

John leant and whispered in Pat's ear, and relief crept into Pat's eyes. The condition had nothing to do with drink and blondes, really nothing to do with him at all.

John began to get in the limousine.

"Goodbye, putative father," he said, almost with affection.

Pat stood looking after him.

"Goodbye son," he said. He stood watching the limousine go out of sight. Then he turned away – feeling like… like Stella Dallas.* There were tears in his eyes.

Potato Father – whatever that meant. After some consideration he added to himself: it's better than not being a father at all.

4

HE AWOKE LATE NEXT AFTERNOON with a happy hangover – the cause of which he could not determine until young John's voice seemed to spring into his ears, repeating:

"Fifty sovereigns a month, with just one condition – that it be withdrawn in case of war, when all revenues of our state will revert to the British Empire."

With a cry Pat sprang to the door. No *Los Angeles Times* lay against it, no *Examiner* – only *Toddy's Daily Form Sheet*. He searched the orange pages frantically. Below the form sheets, the past performances, the endless oracles for endless racetracks, his eye was caught by a one-inch item:

LONDON, SEPTEMBER 3RD. ON THIS MORNING'S DECLARATION BY CHAMBERLAIN, DOUGIE CABLES "ENGLAND TO WIN, FRANCE TO PLACE, RUSSIA TO SHOW".

The Homes of the Stars

B ENEATH A GREAT STRIPED UMBRELLA at the side of
a boulevard in a Hollywood heatwave, sat a man. His
name was Gus Venske (no relation to the runner)* and he
wore magenta pants, cerise shoes and a sport article from
Vine Street which resembled nothing so much as a cerulean-
blue pyjama top.

Gus Venske was not a freak, nor were his clothes at all extraor-
dinary for his time and place. He had a profession – on a pole
beside the umbrella was a placard:

VISIT THE HOMES OF THE STARS

Business was bad or Gus would not have hailed the unprosper-
ous man who stood in the street beside a panting, steaming car,
anxiously watching its efforts to cool.

"Hey fella," said Gus, without much hope. "Wanna visit the
homes of the stars?"

The red-rimmed eyes of the watcher turned from the automobile
and looked superciliously upon Gus.

"I'm *in* pictures," said the man, "I'm in 'em myself."

"Actor?"

"No. Writer."

Pat Hobby turned back to his car, which was whistling like a peanut wagon. He had told the truth – or what was once the truth. Often in the old days his name had flashed on the screen for the few seconds allotted to authorship, but for the past five years his services had been less and less in demand.

Presently Gus Venske shut up shop for lunch by putting his folders and maps into a briefcase and walking off with it under his arm. As the sun grew hotter moment by moment, Pat Hobby took refuge under the faint protection of the umbrella and inspected a soiled folder which had been dropped by Mr Venske. If Pat had not been down to his last fourteen cents he would have telephoned a garage for aid – as it was, he could only wait.

After a while a limousine with a Missouri licence drew to rest beside him. Behind the chauffeur sat a little white moustached man and a large woman with a small dog. They conversed for a moment – then, in a rather shamefaced way, the woman leant out and addressed Pat.

"What stars' homes can you visit?" she asked.

It took a moment for this to sink in.

"I mean, can we go to Robert Taylor's home and Clark Gable's and Shirley Temple's—"

"I guess you can if you can get in," said Pat.

"Because," continued the woman, "if we could go to the very best homes, the most exclusive – we would be prepared to pay more than your regular price."

Light dawned upon Pat. Here together were suckers and smackers. Here was that dearest of Hollywood dreams – the angle. If one got the right angle it meant meals at the Brown Derby, long nights with bottles and girls, a new tyre for his old car. And here was an angle fairly thrusting itself at him.

He rose and went to the side of the limousine.

"Sure. Maybe I could fix it." As he spoke he felt a pang of doubt. "Would you be able to pay in advance?"

The couple exchanged a look.

"Suppose we gave you five dollars now," the woman said, "and five dollars if we can visit Clark Gable's home or somebody like that."

Once upon a time such a thing would have been so easy. In his salad days when Pat had twelve or fifteen writing credits a year, he could have called up many people who would have said, "Sure, Pat, if it means anything to you." But now he could only think of a handful who really recognized him and spoke to him around the lots – Melvyn Douglas and Robert Young and Ronald Colman and Young Doug.* Those he had known best had retired or passed away.

And he did not know except vaguely where the new stars lived, but he had noticed that on the folder were typewritten several dozen names and addresses with pencilled checks after each.

"Of course you can't be sure anybody's at home," he said, "they might be working in the studios."

"We understand that." The lady glanced at Pat's car, glanced away. "We'd better go in our motor."

"Sure."

Pat got up in front with the chauffeur – trying to think fast. The actor who spoke to him most pleasantly was Ronald Colman – they had never exchanged more than conventional salutations, but he might pretend that he was calling to interest Colman in a story.

Better still, Colman was probably not at home and Pat might wangle his clients an inside glimpse of the house. Then the process might be repeated at Robert Young's house and Young Doug's and Melvyn Douglas's. By that time the lady would have forgotten Gable and the afternoon would be over.

He looked at Ronald Colman's address on the folder and gave the direction to the chauffeur.

"We know a woman who had her picture taken with George Brent,"* said the lady as they started off, "Mrs Horace J. Ives, Jr."

"She's our neighbour," said her husband. "She lives at 372 Rose Drive in Kansas City. And we live at 327."

"She had her picture taken with George Brent. We always wondered if she had to pay for it. Of course I don't know that I'd want to go so far as *that*. I don't know what they'd say back home."

"I don't think we want to go as far as all that," agreed her husband.

"Where are we going first?" asked the lady, cosily.

"Well, I had a couple calls to pay anyhow," said Pat. "I got to see Ronald Colman about something."

"Oh, he's one of my favourites. Do you know him well?"

"Oh yes," said Pat, "I'm not in this business regularly. I'm just doing it today for a friend. I'm a writer."

Sure in the knowledge that not so much as a trio of picture writers were known to the public he named himself as the author of several recent successes.

"That's very interesting," said the man, "I knew a writer once – this Upton Sinclair or Sinclair Lewis.* Not a bad fellow even if he was a socialist."

"Why aren't you writing a picture now?" asked the lady.

"Well, you see, we're on strike," Pat invented. "We got a thing called the Screen Playwriters' Guild and we're on strike."

"Oh." His clients stared with suspicion at this emissary of Stalin in the front seat of their car.

"What are you striking for?" asked the man uneasily.

Pat's political development was rudimentary. He hesitated.

"Oh, better living conditions," he said finally, "free pencils and paper. I don't know – it's all in the Wagner Act."* After a moment he added vaguely, "Recognize Finland."

"I didn't know writers had unions," said the man. "Well, if you're on strike, who writes the movies?"

"The producers," said Pat bitterly. "That's why they're so lousy."

"Well, that's what I would call an odd state of things."

They came in sight of Ronald Colman's house and Pat swallowed uneasily. A shining new roadster sat out in front.

"I better go in first," he said. "I mean we wouldn't want to come in on any... on any family scene or anything."

"Does he have family scenes?" asked the lady eagerly.

"Oh, well, you know how people are," said Pat with charity. "I think I ought to see how things are first."

The car stopped. Drawing a long breath, Pat got out. At the same moment the door of the house opened and Ronald Colman hurried down the walk. Pat's heart missed a beat as the actor glanced in his direction.

"Hello Pat," he said. Evidently he had no notion that Pat was a caller, for he jumped into his car and the sound of his motor drowned out Pat's responses as he drove away.

"Well, he called you 'Pat'," said the woman, impressed.

"I guess he was in a hurry," said Pat. "But maybe we could see his house."

He rehearsed a speech going up the walk. He had just spoken to his friend Mr Colman, and received permission to look around.

But the house was shut and locked and there was no answer to the bell. He would have to try Melvyn Douglas, whose salutations, on second thought, were a little warmer than Ronald Colman's. At any rate his clients' faith in him was now firmly founded. The "Hello, Pat" rang confidently in their ears; by proxy they were already inside the charmed circle.

"Now let's try Clark Gable's," said the lady. "I'd like to tell Carole Lombard about her hair."

The lese-majesty made Pat's stomach wince. Once in a crowd he had met Clark Gable, but he had no reason to believe that Mr Gable remembered.

"Well, we could try Melvyn Douglas's first and then Bob Young or else Young Doug. They're all on the way. You see Gable and Lombard live away out in the San Joaquin Valley."

"Oh," said the lady, disappointed, "I did want to run up and see their bedroom. Well then, our next choice would be Shirley

Temple." She looked at her little dog. "I know that would be Boojie's choice too."

"They're kind of afraid of kidnappers," said Pat.

Ruffled, the man produced his business card and handed it to Pat.

DEERING R. ROBINSON
Vice President and Chairman
of the Board
Robdeer Food Products

"Does *that* sound as if I want to kidnap Shirley Temple?"

"They just have to be sure," said Pat apologetically. "After we go to Melvyn—"

"No – let's see Shirley Temple's *now*," insisted the woman. "Really! I told you in the first place what I wanted."

Pat hesitated.

"First I'll have to stop in some drugstore and phone about it."

In a drugstore he exchanged some of the five dollars for a half-pint of gin and took two long swallows behind a high counter, after which he considered the situation. He could, of course, duck Mr and Mrs Robinson immediately – after all he had produced Ronald Colman, with sound, for their five smackers. On the other hand they just *might* catch Miss Temple on her way in or out – and for a pleasant day at Santa Anita tomorrow Pat needed five smackers more. In the glow of the gin his courage mounted, and returning to the limousine he gave the chauffeur the address.

But approaching the Temple house his spirit quailed as he saw that there was a tall iron fence and an electric gate. And didn't guides have to have a licence?

"Not here," he said quickly to the chauffeur. "I made a mistake. I think it's the next one, or two or three doors further on."

He decided on a large mansion set in an open lawn and, stopping the chauffeur, got out and walked up to the door. He was temporarily licked, but at least he might bring back some story to soften them – say, that Miss Temple had mumps. He could point out her sickroom from the walk.

There was no answer to his ring, but he saw that the door was partly ajar. Cautiously he pushed it open. He was staring into a deserted living room on the baronial scale. He listened. There was no one about, no footsteps on the upper floor, no murmur from the kitchen. Pat took another pull at the gin. Then swiftly he hurried back to the limousine.

"She's at the studio," he said quickly. "But if we're quiet we can look at their living room."

Eagerly the Robinsons and Boojie disembarked and followed him. The living room might have been Shirley Temple's, might have been one of many in Hollywood. Pat saw a doll in a corner and pointed at it, whereupon Mrs Robinson picked it up, looked at it reverently and showed it to Boojie, who sniffed indifferently.

"Could I meet Mrs Temple?" she asked.

"Oh, she's out – nobody's home," Pat said – unwisely.

"Nobody. Oh – then Boojie would so like a wee little peep at her bedroom."

Before he could answer she had run up the stairs. Mr Robinson followed and Pat waited uneasily in the hall, ready to depart at the sound either of an arrival outside or a commotion above.

He finished the bottle, disposed of it politely under a sofa cushion and then, deciding that the visit upstairs was tempting fate too far, he went after his clients. On the stairs he heard Mrs Robinson.

"But there's only *one* child's bedroom. I thought Shirley had brothers."

A window on the winding staircase looked upon the street, and glancing out Pat saw a large car drive up to the kerb. From it stepped a Hollywood celebrity who, though not one of those pursued by Mrs Robinson, was second to none in prestige and power. It was old Mr Marcus, the producer, for whom Pat Hobby had been press agent twenty years ago.

At this point Pat lost his head. In a flash he pictured an elaborate explanation as to what he was doing here. He would not be forgiven. His occasional weeks in the studio at two fifty would now disappear altogether and another finis would be written to his almost entirely finished career. He left, impetuously and swiftly – down the stairs, through the kitchen and out the back gate, leaving the Robinsons to their destiny.

Vaguely he was sorry for them as he walked quickly along the next boulevard. He could see Mr Robinson producing his card as the head of Robdeer Food Products. He could see Mr Marcus's scepticism, the arrival of the police, the frisking of Mr and Mrs Robinson.

Probably it would stop there – except that the Robinsons would be furious at him for his imposition. They would tell the police where they had picked him up.

Suddenly he went ricketing down the street, beads of gin breaking out profusely on his forehead. He had left his car beside Gus Venske's umbrella. And now he remembered another recognizing clue and hoped that Ronald Colman didn't know his last name.

Pat Hobby Does His Bit

1

IN ORDER TO BORROW MONEY gracefully one must choose the time and place. It is a difficult business, for example, when the borrower is cockeyed, or has measles, or a conspicuous shiner. One could continue indefinitely, but the inauspicious occasions can be catalogued as one – it is exceedingly difficult to borrow money when one needs it.

Pat Hobby found it difficult in the case of an actor on a set during the shooting of a moving picture. It was about the stiffest chore he had ever undertaken, but he was doing it to save his car. To a sordidly commercial glance the jalopy would not have seemed worth saving, but because of Hollywood's great distances it was an indispensable tool of the writer's trade.

"The finance company—" explained Pat, but Gyp McCarthy interrupted.

"I got some business in this next take. You want me to blow up on it?"

"I only need twenty," persisted Pat. "I can't get jobs if I have to hang around my bedroom."

"You'd save money that way – you don't get jobs any more."

This was cruelly correct. But, working or not, Pat liked to pass his days in or near a studio. He had reached a dolorous and precarious forty-nine with nothing else to do.

"I got a rewrite job promised for next week," he lied.

"Oh, nuts to you," said Gyp. "You better get off the set before Hilliard sees you."

Pat glanced nervously towards the group by the camera – then he played his trump card.

"Once," he said, "once I paid for you to have a baby."

"Sure you did!" said Gyp wrathfully. "That was sixteen years ago. And where is it now? It's in jail for running over an old lady without a licence."

"Well I paid for it," said Pat. "Two hundred smackers."

"That's nothing to what it cost me. Would I be stunting at my age if I had dough to lend? Would I be working at all?"

From somewhere in the darkness, an assistant director issued an order:

"Ready to go!"

Pat spoke quickly.

"All right," he said. "Five bucks."

"No."

"All right then," Pat's red-rimmed eyes tightened. "I'm going to stand over there and put the hex on you while you say your line."

"Oh, for God's sake!" said Gyp uneasily. "Listen, I'll give you five. It's in my coat over there. Here, I'll get it."

He dashed from the set and Pat heaved a sigh of relief. Maybe Louie, the studio bookie, would let him have ten more.

Again the assistant director's voice:

"Quiet!... We'll take it now!... Lights!"

The glare stabbed into Pat's eyes, blinding him. He took a step the wrong way – then back. Six other people were in the take – a gangster's hideout – and it seemed that each was in his way.

"All right... Roll 'em... We're turning!"

In his panic, Pat had stepped behind a flat which would effectually conceal him. While the actors played their scene he stood there trembling a little, his back hunched – quite unaware that it was a "trolley shot", that the camera, moving forward on its track, was almost upon him.

"You by the window – hey you, *Gyp*! Hands up."

Like a man in a dream, Pat raised his hands – only then did he realize that he was looking directly into a great black lens – in an instant it also included the English leading woman, who ran past him and jumped out the window. After an interminable second, Pat heard the order "Cut".

Then he rushed blindly through a property door, around a corner, tripping over a cable, recovering himself and tearing for the entrance. He heard footsteps running behind him and increased his gait, but in the doorway itself he was overtaken and turned defensively.

It was the English actress.

"Hurry up!" she cried. "That finishes my work. I'm flying home to England."

As she scrambled into her waiting limousine, she threw back a last irrelevant remark. "I'm catching a New York plane in an hour."

"Who cares!" Pat thought bitterly, as he scurried away.

He was unaware that her repatriation was to change the course of his life.

2

AND HE DID NOT HAVE THE FIVE – he feared that this particular five was forever out of range. Other means must be found to keep the wolf from the two doors of his coupé. Pat left the lot with despair in his heart, stopping only momentarily to get gas for the car and gin for himself, possibly the last of many drinks they had had together.

Next morning he awoke with an aggravated problem. For once he did not want to go to the studio. It was not merely Gyp McCarthy he feared – it was the whole corporate might of a moving-picture company, nay of an industry. Actually to have interfered with the shooting of a movie was somehow a major delinquency, compared to which expensive fumblings on the part of producers or writers went comparatively unpunished.

On the other hand, zero hour for the car was the day after tomorrow, and Louie, the studio bookie, seemed positively the last resource, and a poor one at that.

Nerving himself with an unpalatable snack from the bottom of the bottle, he went to the studio at ten with his coat collar turned up and his hat pulled low over his ears. He knew a sort of underground railway through the make-up department and the commissary kitchen which might get him to Louie's suite unobserved.

Two studio policemen seized him as he rounded the corner by the barber shop.

"Hey, I got a pass!" he protested. "Good for a week – signed by Jack Berners."

"Mr Berners specially wants to see you."

Here it was then – he would be barred from the lot.

"We could sue you!" cried Jack Berners. "But we couldn't recover."

"What's one take?" demanded Pat. "You can use another."

"No we can't – the camera jammed. And this morning Lily Keatts took a plane to England. She thought she was through."

"Cut the scene," suggested Pat – and then, on inspiration: "I bet I could fix it for you."

"You fixed it, all right!" Berners assured him. "If there was any way to fix it back I wouldn't have sent for you."

He paused, looked speculatively at Pat. His buzzer sounded and a secretary's voice said, "Mr Hilliard."

"Send him in."

George Hilliard was a huge man, and the glance he bent upon Pat was not kindly. But there was some other element besides anger in it, and Pat squirmed doubtfully as the two men regarded him with almost impersonal curiosity – as if he were a candidate for a cannibal's frying pan.

"Well, goodbye," he suggested uneasily.

"What do you think, George?" demanded Berners.

"Well…" said Hilliard, hesitantly, "we could black out a couple of teeth."

Pat rose hurriedly and took a step towards the door, but Hilliard seized him and faced him around.

"Let's hear you talk," he said.

"You can't beat me up," Pat clamoured. "You knock my teeth out and I'll sue you."

There was a pause.

"What do you think?" demanded Berners.

"He can't talk," said Hilliard.

"You damn right I can talk!" said Pat.

"We can dub three or four lines," continued Hilliard, "and nobody'll know the difference. Half the guys you get to play rats can't talk. The point is this one's got the physique and the camera will pull it out of his face too."

Berners nodded.

"All right, Pat – you're an actor. You've got to play the part this McCarthy had. Only a couple of scenes, but they're important. You'll have papers to sign with the Guild and Central Casting and you can report for work this afternoon."

"What is this?" Pat demanded. "I'm no ham…" Remembering that Hilliard had once been a leading man he recoiled from this attitude: "I'm a writer."

"The character you play is called 'The Rat'," continued Berners. He explained why it was necessary for Pat to continue his impromptu appearance of yesterday. The scenes which included Miss Keatts had been shot first, so that she could fulfil an English engagement. But in the filling-out of the skeleton it was necessary to show how the gangsters reached their hideout, and what they did after Miss Keatts dove from the window. Having irrevocably appeared in the shot with Miss Keatts, Pat must appear in half a dozen other shots, to be taken in the next few days.

"What kind of jack is it?" Pat enquired.

"We were paying McCarthy fifty a day – wait a minute Pat – but I thought I'd pay you your last writing price, two fifty for the week."

"How about my reputation?" objected Pat.

"I won't answer that one," said Berners. "But if Benchley can act and Don Stuart and Lewis and Wilder and Woollcott, I guess it won't ruin you."*

Pat drew a long breath.

"Can you let me have fifty on account?" he asked. "Because really I earned that yester—"

"If you got what you earned yesterday you'd be in a hospital. And you're not going on any bat. Here's ten dollars and that's all you see for a week."

"How about my car—"

"To hell with your car."

3

"THE RAT" WAS THE DIE-HARD of the gang who were engaged in sabotage for an unidentified government of N-zis. His speeches were simplicity itself – Pat had written their like many times. "Don't finish him till the Brain comes"; "Let's get out of here"; "Fella, you're going out feet first". Pat found it pleasant – mostly waiting around as in all picture work – and he hoped it might lead to other openings in this line. He was sorry that the job was so short.

His last scene was on location. He knew "The Rat" was to touch off an explosion in which he himself was killed, but Pat had watched such scenes and was certain he would be in no slightest danger. Out on the back lot, he was mildly curious when they measured him around the waist and chest.

"Making a dummy?" he asked.

"Not exactly," the prop man said. "This thing is all made, but it was for Gyp McCarthy and I want to see if it'll fit you."

"Does it?"

"Just exactly."

"What is it?"

"Well – it's a sort of protector."

A slight draught of uneasiness blew in Pat's mind.

"Protector for what? Against the explosion?"

"Heck no! The explosion is phoney – just a process shot. This is something else."

"What is it?" persisted Pat. "If I got to be protected against something, I got a right to know what it is."

Near the false front of a warehouse, a battery of cameras were getting into position. George Hilliard came suddenly out of a group and towards Pat and, putting his arm on his shoulder, steered him toward the actors' dressing tent. Once inside, he handed Pat a flask.

"Have a drink, old man."

Pat took a long pull.

"There's a bit of business, Pat," Hilliard said, "needs some new costuming. I'll explain it while they dress you."

Pat was divested of coat and vest, his trousers were loosened, and in an instant a hinged iron doublet was fastened about his middle, extending from his armpits to his crotch very much like a plaster cast.

"This is the very finest strongest iron, Pat," Hilliard assured him. "The very best in tensile strength and resistance. It was built in Pittsburgh."

Pat suddenly resisted the attempts of two dressers to pull his trousers up over the thing and to slip on his coat and vest.

"What's it for?" he demanded, arms flailing. "I want to know. You're not going to shoot at me if that's what—"

"No shooting."

"Then what *is* it? I'm no stuntman—"

"You signed a contract just like McCarthy's to do anything within reason – and our lawyers have certified this."

"What *is* it?" Pat's mouth was dry.

"It's an automobile."

"You're going to hit me with an automobile."

"Give me a chance to tell you," begged Hilliard. "Nobody's going to hit you. The auto's going to pass over you, that's all. This case is so strong—"

"Oh no!" said Pat. "Oh no!" He tore at the iron corselet. "Not on your—"

George Hilliard pinioned his arms firmly.

"Pat, you almost wrecked this picture once – you're not going to do it again. Be a man."

"That's what I'm going to be. You're not going to squash me out flat like that extra last month."

He broke off. Behind Hilliard he saw a face he knew – a hateful and dreaded face – that of the collector for the North Hollywood Finance and Loan Company. Over in the parking lot stood his coupé, faithful pal and servant since 1934, companion of his misfortunes, his only certain home.

"Either you fill your contract," said George Hilliard, "or you're out of pictures for keeps."

The man from the finance company had taken a step forward. Pat turned to Hilliard.

"Will you loan me…" he faltered, "will you advance me twenty-five dollars?"

"Sure," said Hilliard.

Pat spoke fiercely to the credit man:

"You hear that? You'll get your money, but if this thing breaks, my death'll be on your head."

The next few minutes passed in a dream. He heard Hilliard's last instructions as they walked from the tent. Pat was to be lying in a shallow ditch to touch off the dynamite – and then the hero would drive the car slowly across his middle. Pat listened dimly. A picture of himself, cracked like an egg by the factory wall, lay athwart his mind.

He picked up the torch and lay down in the ditch. Afar off he heard the call "Quiet", then Hilliard's voice and the noise of the car warming up.

"Action!" called someone. There was the sound of the car growing nearer – louder. And then Pat Hobby knew no more.

4

W HEN HE AWOKE it was dark and quiet. For some moments he failed to recognize his whereabouts. Then he saw that stars were out in the California sky and that he was somewhere alone – no – he was held tight in someone's arms. But the arms were of iron and he realized that he was still in the metallic casing. And then it all came back to him – up to the moment when he heard the approach of the car.

As far as he could determine he was unhurt – but why out here and alone?

He struggled to get up, but found it was impossible, and after a horrified moment he let out a cry for help. For five minutes he called out at intervals until finally a voice came from far away, and assistance arrived in the form of a studio policeman.

"What is it fella? A drop too much?"

"Hell no," cried Pat. "I was in the shooting this afternoon. It was a lousy trick to go off and leave me in this ditch."

"They must have forgot you in the excitement."

"Forgot me! *I* was the excitement. If you don't believe me then feel what I got on!"

The cop helped him to his feet.

"They was upset," he explained. "A star don't break his leg every day."

"What's that? Did something happen?"

"Well, as I heard, he was supposed to drive the car at a bump and the car turned over and broke his leg. They had to stop shooting and they're all kind of gloomy."

"And they leave me inside this... this stove. How do I get it off tonight? How'm I going to drive my car?"

But for all his rage Pat felt a certain fierce pride. He was Something in this set-up – someone to be reckoned with after years of neglect. He had managed to hold up the picture once more.

Pat Hobby's Preview

1

"I HAVEN'T GOT A JOB FOR YOU," said Berners. "We've got more writers now than we can use."

"I didn't ask for a job," said Pat with dignity. "But I rate some tickets for the preview tonight – since I got a half-credit."

"Oh yes, I want to talk to you about that," Berners frowned. "We may have to take your name off the screen credits."

"*What?*" exclaimed Pat. "Why, it's already on! I saw it in the *Reporter.* "By Ward Wainwright and Pat Hobby."'

"But we may have to take it off when we release the picture. Wainwright's back from the East and raising hell. He says that you claimed lines where all you did was change 'No' to 'No, sir' and 'crimson' to 'red', and stuff like that."

"I been in this business twenty years," said Pat. "I know my rights. That guy laid an egg. I was called in to revise a turkey!"

"You were not," Berners assured him. "After Wainwright went to New York I called you in to fix one small character. If I hadn't gone fishing you wouldn't have got away with sticking your name on the script." Jack Berners broke off, touched by Pat's dismal red-streaked eyes. "Still, I was glad to see you get a credit after so long."

"I'll join the Screen Writers' Guild and fight it."

"You don't stand a chance. Anyhow, Pat, your name's on it tonight at least, and it'll remind everybody you're alive. And I'll dig you up some tickets – but keep an eye out for Wainwright. It isn't good for you to get socked if you're over fifty."

"I'm in my forties," said Pat, who was forty-nine.

The Dictograph buzzed. Berners switched it on.

"It's Mr Wainwright."

"Tell him to wait." He turned to Pat: "That's Wainwright. Better go out the side door."

"How about the tickets?"

"Drop by this afternoon."

To a rising young screen poet this might have been a crushing blow, but Pat was made of sterner stuff. Sterner not upon himself, but on the harsh fate that had dogged him for nearly a decade. With all his experience, and with the help of every poisonous herb that blossoms between Washington Boulevard and Ventura, between Santa Monica and Vine – he continued to slip. Sometimes he grabbed momentarily at a bush, found a few weeks' surcease upon the island of a "patch job", but in general the slide continued at a pace that would have dizzied a lesser man.

Once safely out of Berners's office, for instance, Pat looked ahead and not behind. He visioned a drink with Louie, the studio bookie, and then a call on some old friends on the lot. Occasionally, but less often every year, some of these calls developed into jobs before you could say "Santa Anita". But after he had had his drink his eyes fell upon a lost girl.

She was obviously lost. She stood staring very prettily at the trucks full of extras that rolled towards the commissary. And then gazed about helpless – so helpless that a truck was almost upon her when Pat reached out and plucked her aside.

"Oh, thanks," she said, "thanks. I came with a party for a tour of the studio, and a policeman made me leave my camera in some office. Then I went to Stage 5 where the guide said, but it was closed."

She was a "Cute Little Blonde". To Pat's liverish eye, cute little blondes seemed as much alike as a string of paper dolls. Of course they had different names.

"We'll see about it," said Pat.

"You're very nice. I'm Eleanor Carter from Boise, Idaho."

He told her his name and that he was a writer. She seemed first disappointed – then delighted.

"A writer?... Oh, of course. I knew they had to have writers, but I guess I never heard about one before."

"Writers get as much as three grand a week," he assured her firmly. "Writers are some of the biggest shots in Hollywood."

"You see, I never thought of it that way."

"Bernud Shaw was out here," he said, "and Einstein, but they couldn't make the grade."

They walked to the Bulletin Board and Pat found that there was work scheduled on three stages – and one of the directors was a friend out of the past.

"What did you write?" Eleanor asked.

A great male Star loomed on the horizon and Eleanor was all eyes till he had passed. Anyhow, the names of Pat's pictures would have been unfamiliar to her.

"Those were all silents," he said.

"Oh. Well, what did you write last?"

"Well, I worked on a thing at Universal – I don't know what they called it finally..." He saw that he was not impressing her at all. He thought quickly. What did they know in Boise, Idaho? "I wrote *Captains Courageous*," he said boldly. "And *Test Pilot* and *Wuthering Heights* and... and *The Awful Truth* and *Mr Smith Goes to Washington*."*

"Oh!" she exclaimed. "Those are all my favourite pictures. And *Test Pilot* is my boyfriend's favourite picture and *Dark Victory* is mine."

"I thought *Dark Victory* stank," he said modestly. "Highbrow stuff." And he added, to balance the scales of truth, "I been here twenty years."

They came to a stage and went in. Pat sent his name to the director and they were passed. They watched while Ronald Colman rehearsed a scene.

"Did you write this?" Eleanor whispered.

"They asked me to," Pat said, "but I was busy."

He felt young again, authoritative and active, with a hand in many schemes. Then he remembered something.

"I've got a picture opening tonight."

"You *have*?"

He nodded.

"I was going to take Claudette Colbert, but she's got a cold. Would you like to go?"

2

H<small>E WAS ALARMED</small> when she mentioned a family, relieved when she said it was only a resident aunt. It would be like old times walking with a cute little blonde past the staring crowds on the sidewalk. His car was Class of 1933, but he could say it was borrowed – one of his Jap servants had smashed his limousine. Then what? he didn't quite know, but he could put on a good act for one night.

He bought her lunch in the commissary and was so stirred that he thought of borrowing somebody's apartment for the day. There was the old line about "getting her a test". But Eleanor was thinking only of getting to a hairdresser to prepare for tonight, and he escorted her reluctantly to the gate. He had another drink with Louie and went to Jack Berners's office for the tickets.

Berners's secretary had them ready in an envelope.

"We had trouble about these, Mr Hobby."

"Trouble? Why? Can't a man go to his own preview? Is this something new?"

"It's not that, Mr Hobby," she said. "The picture's been talked about so much, every seat is gone."

Unreconciled, he complained, "And they just didn't think of me."

"I'm sorry." She hesitated. "These are really Mr Wainwright's tickets. He was so angry about something that he said he wouldn't go – and threw them on my desk. I shouldn't be telling you this."

"These are *his* seats?"

"Yes, Mr Hobby."

Pat sucked his tongue. This was in the nature of a triumph. Wainwright had lost his temper, which was the last thing you should ever do in pictures – you could only pretend to lose it – so perhaps his apple cart wasn't so steady. Perhaps Pat ought to join the Screen Writers' Guild and present his case – if the Screen Writers' Guild would take him in.

This problem was academic. He was calling for Eleanor at five o'clock and taking her "somewhere for a cocktail". He bought a two-dollar shirt, changing into it in the shop, and a four-dollar Alpine hat – thus halving his bank account, which, since the Bank Holiday of 1933,* he carried cautiously in his pocket.

The modest bungalow in West Hollywood yielded up Eleanor without a struggle. On his advice she was not in evening dress, but she was as trim and shining as any cute little blonde out of his past. Eager too – running over with enthusiasm and gratitude. He must think of someone whose apartment he could borrow for tomorrow.

"You'd like a test?" he asked as they entered the Brown Derby bar.

"What girl wouldn't?"

"Some wouldn't – for a million dollars." Pat had had setbacks in his love life. "Some of them would rather go on pounding the keys or just hanging around. You'd be surprised."

"I'd do almost anything for a test," Eleanor said.

Looking at her two hours later, he wondered honestly to himself if it couldn't be arranged. There was Harry Gooddorf – there was Jack Berners – but his credit was low on all sides. He could do *something* for her, he decided. He would try at least to get an agent interested – if all went well tomorrow.

"What are you doing tomorrow?" he asked.

"Nothing," she answered promptly. "Hadn't we better eat and get to the preview?"

"Sure, sure."

He made a further inroad on his bank account to pay for his six whiskeys – you certainly had the right to celebrate before your own preview – and took her into the restaurant for dinner. They ate little. Eleanor was too excited – Pat had taken his calories in another form.

It was a long time since he had seen a picture with his name on it. Pat Hobby. As a man of the people he always appeared in the credit titles as Pat Hobby. It would be nice to see it again, and though he did not expect his old friends to stand up and sing 'Happy Birthday to You', he was sure there would be back-slapping and even a little turn of attention towards him as the crowd swayed out of the theatre. That would be nice.

"I'm frightened," said Eleanor as they walked through the alley of packed fans.

"They're looking at you," he said confidently. "They look at that pretty pan and try to think if you're an actress."

A fan shoved an autograph album and pencil towards Eleanor, but Pat moved her firmly along. It was late – the equivalent of "all aboard" was being shouted around the entrance.

"Show your tickets, please, sir."

Pat opened the envelope and handed them to the doorman. Then he said to Eleanor:

"The seats are reserved – it doesn't matter that we're late."

She pressed close to him, clinging – it was, as it turned out, the high point of her debut. Less than three steps inside the theatre, a hand fell on Pat's shoulder.

"Hey buddy, these aren't tickets for here."

Before they knew it, they were back outside the door, glared at with suspicious eyes.

"I'm Pat Hobby. I wrote this picture."

For an instant credulity wandered to his side. Then the hard-boiled doorman sniffed at Pat and stepped in close.

"Buddy, you're drunk. These are tickets to another show."

Eleanor looked and felt uneasy, but Pat was cool.

"Go inside and ask Jack Berners," Pat said. "He'll tell you."

"Now listen," said the husky guard, "these are tickets for a burlesque down in LA." He was steadily edging Pat to the side. "You go to your show, you and your girlfriend. And be happy."

"You don't understand. I wrote this picture."

"Sure. In a pipe dream."

"Look at the programme. My name's on it. I'm Pat Hobby."

"Can you prove it? Let's see your auto licence."

As Pat handed it over, he whispered to Eleanor, "Don't worry!"

"This doesn't say Pat Hobby," announced the doorman. "This says the car's owned by the North Hollywood Finance and Loan Company. Is that you?"

For once in his life, Pat could think of nothing to say – he cast one quick glance at Eleanor. Nothing in her face indicated that he was anything but what he thought he was – all alone.

3

THOUGH THE PREVIEW CROWD had begun to drift away, with that vague American wonder as to why they had come at all, one little cluster found something arresting and poignant in the faces of Pat and Eleanor. They were obviously gatecrashers, outsiders like themselves, but the crowd resented the temerity of their effort to get in – a temerity which the crowd did not share. Little jeering jests were audible. Then, with Eleanor already edging away from the distasteful scene, there was a flurry by the door. A well-dressed six-footer strode out of the theatre and stood gazing till he saw Pat.

"There you are!" he shouted.

Pat recognized Ward Wainwright.

"Go in and look at it!" Wainwright roared. "Look at it. Here's some ticket stubs! I think the prop boy directed it! Go and look!" To the doorman he said: "It's all right! *He* wrote it. I wouldn't have my name on an inch of it."

Trembling with frustration, Wainwright threw up his hands and strode off into the curious crowd.

Eleanor was terrified. But the same spirit that had inspired "I'd do anything to get in the movies" kept her standing there – though she felt invisible fingers reaching forth to drag her back to Boise. She had been intending to run – hard and fast. The hard-boiled doorman and the tall stranger had crystallized her feelings that Pat was "rather simple". She would never let those red-rimmed eyes come close to her – at least for any more than a doorstep kiss. She was saving herself for somebody – and it wasn't Pat. Yet she felt that the lingering crowd was a tribute to her – such as she had never exacted before. Several times she threw a glance at the crowd – a glance that now changed from wavering fear into a sort of queenliness.

She felt exactly like a star.

Pat, too, was all confidence. This was *his* preview; all had been delivered into his hands: his name would stand alone on the screen when the picture was released. There had to be somebody's name – didn't there? – and Wainwright had withdrawn.

SCREENPLAY BY PAT HOBBY.

He seized Eleanor's elbow in a firm grasp and steered her triumphantly towards the door:

"Cheer up, baby. That's the way it is. You see?"

No Harm Trying

1

P AT HOBBY'S APARTMENT lay athwart a delicatessen shop
on Wilshire Boulevard. And there lay Pat himself, surrounded
by his books – the *Motion Picture Almanac* of 1928 and *Barton's
Track Guide, 1939* – by his pictures, authentically signed photo-
graphs of Mabel Normand and Barbara La Marr* (who, being
deceased, had no value in the pawnshops) – and by his dogs in
their cracked leather oxfords, perched on the arm of a slanting
settee.

Pat was at "the end of his resources" – though this term is too
ominous to describe a fairly usual condition in his life. He was
an old-timer in pictures; he had once known sumptuous living,
but for the past ten years jobs had been hard to hold – harder to
hold than glasses.

"Think of it," he often mourned. "Only a writer – at forty-nine."

All this afternoon he had turned the pages of *The Times* and
The Examiner for an idea. Though he did not intend to compose
a motion picture from this idea, he needed it to get him inside a
studio. If you had nothing to submit, it was increasingly difficult
to pass the gate. But though these two newspapers, together with
Life, were the sources most commonly combed for "originals",

they yielded him nothing this afternoon. There were wars, a fire in Topanga Canyon, press releases from the studios, municipal corruptions and always the redeeming deeds of "The Trojuns",* but Pat found nothing that competed in human interest with the betting page.

"If I could get out to Santa Anita," he thought, "I could maybe get an idea about the nags."

This cheering idea was interrupted by his landlord, from the delicatessen store below.

"I told you I wouldn't deliver any more messages," said Nick, "and *still* I won't. But Mr Carl Le Vigne is telephoning in person from the studio and wants you should go over right away."

The prospect of a job did something to Pat. It anaesthetized the crumbled, struggling remnants of his manhood and inoculated him instead with a bland, easy-going confidence. The set speeches and attitudes of success returned to him. His manner as he winked at a studio policeman, stopped to chat with Louie, the bookie, and presented himself to Mr Le Vigne's secretary indicated that he had been engaged with momentous tasks in other parts of the globe. By saluting Le Vigne with a facetious "Hel-*lo* Captain!" he behaved almost as an equal, a trusted lieutenant who had never really been away.

"Pat, your wife's in the hospital," Le Vigne said. "It'll probably be in the papers this afternoon."

Pat started.

"My wife?" he said. "What wife?"

"Estelle. She tried to cut her wrists."

"Estelle!" Pat exclaimed. "You mean *Estelle*? Say, I was only married to her three weeks!"

"She was the best girl you ever had," said Le Vigne grimly.

"I haven't even heard of her for ten years."

"You're hearing about her now. They called all the studios trying to locate you."

"I had nothing to do with it."

"I know – she's only been here a week. She had a run of hard luck wherever it was she lived – New Orleans? Husband died, child died, no money…"

Pat breathed easier. They weren't trying to hang anything on him.

"Anyhow she'll live," Le Vigne reassured him superfluously, "and she was the best script girl on the lot once. We'd like to take care of her. We thought the way was give you a job. Not exactly a job, because I know you're not up to it." He glanced into Pat's red-rimmed eyes. "More of a sinecure."

Pat became uneasy. He didn't recognize the word, but "sin" disturbed him and "cure" brought a whole flood of unpleasant memories.

"You're on the payroll at two fifty a week for three weeks," said Le Vigne, "but one fifty of that goes to the hospital for your wife's bill."

"But we're divorced!" Pat protested. "No Mexican stuff either. I've been married since, and so has—"

"Take it or leave it. You can have an office here, and if anything you can do comes up we'll let you know."

"I never worked for a hundred a week."

"We're not asking you to work. If you want you can stay home."

Pat reversed his field.

"Oh, I'll work," he said quickly. "You dig me up a good story and I'll show you whether I can work or not."

Le Vigne wrote something on a slip of paper.

"All right. They'll find you an office."

Outside Pat looked at the memorandum.

"Mrs John Devlin" – it read – "Good Samaritan Hospital."

The very words irritated him.

"Good Samaritan!" he exclaimed. "Good gyp joint! One hundred and fifty bucks a week."

2

PAT HAD BEEN GIVEN many a charity job, but this was the first one that made him feel ashamed. He did not mind not earning his salary, but not getting it was another matter. And he wondered if other people on the lot who were obviously doing nothing were being fairly paid for it. There were, for example, a number of beautiful young ladies who walked aloof as stars, and whom Pat took for stock girls, until Eric, the call boy, told him they were imports from Vienna and Budapest, not yet cast for pictures. Did half their pay cheques go to keep husbands they had only had for three weeks?

The loveliest of these was Lizzette Starheim, a violet-eyed little blonde with an ill-concealed air of disillusion. Pat saw her alone at tea almost every afternoon in the commissary

– and made her acquaintance one day by simply sliding into a chair opposite.

"Hello, Lizzette," he said. "I'm Pat Hobby, the writer."

"Oh, hello!"

She flashed such a dazzling smile that for a moment he thought she must have heard of him.

"When they going to cast you?" he demanded.

"I don't know." Her accent was faint and poignant.

"Don't let them give you the run-around. Not with a face like yours." Her beauty roused a rusty eloquence. "Sometimes they just keep you under contract till your teeth fall out, because you look too much like their big star."

"Oh no," she said distressfully.

"Oh yes!" he assured her. "I'm telling *you*. Why don't you go to another company and get borrowed? Have you thought of that idea?"

"I think it's wonderful."

He intended to go further into the subject, but Miss Starheim looked at her watch and got up.

"I must go now, Mr—"

"Hobby. Pat Hobby."

Pat joined Dutch Waggoner, the director, who was shooting dice with a waitress at another table.

"Between pictures, Dutch?"

"Between pictures hell!" said Dutch. "I haven't done a picture for six months and my contract's got six months to run. I'm trying to break it. Who was the little blonde?"

Afterwards, back in his office, Pat discussed these encounters with Eric the call boy.

"All signed up and no place to go," said Eric. "Look at this Jeff Manfred, now – an associate producer! Sits in his office and sends notes to the big shots – and I carry back word they're in Palm Springs. It breaks my heart. Yesterday he put his head on his desk and boohooed."

"What's the answer?" asked Pat.

"Changea management," suggested Eric, darkly. "Shake-up coming."

"Who's going to the top?" Pat asked, with scarcely concealed excitement.

"Nobody knows," said Eric. "But wouldn't I like to land uphill! Boy! I want a writer's job. I got three ideas so new they're wet behind the ears."

"It's no life at all," Pat assured him with conviction. "I'd trade with you right now."

In the hall next day he intercepted Jeff Manfred, who walked with the unconvincing hurry of one without a destination.

"What's the rush, Jeff?" Pat demanded, falling into step.

"Reading some scripts," Jeff panted without conviction.

Pat drew him unwillingly into his office.

"Jeff, have you heard about the shake-up?"

"Listen now, Pat…" Jeff looked nervously at the walls. "What shake-up?" he demanded.

"I heard that this Harmon Shaver is going to be the new boss," ventured Pat, "Wall Street control."

"Harmon Shaver!" Jeff scoffed. "He doesn't know anything about pictures – he's just a money man. He wanders around like a lost soul." Jeff sat back and considered. "Still – if you're *right*, he'd be a man you could get to." He turned mournful eyes on Pat. "I haven't been able to see Le Vigne or Barnes or Bill Behrer for a month. Can't get an assignment, can't get an actor, can't get a story." He broke off. "I've thought of drumming up something on my own. Got any ideas?"

"Have I?" said Pat. "I got three ideas so new they're wet behind the ears."

"Who for?"

"Lizzette Starheim," said Pat, "with Dutch Waggoner directing – see?"

3

"I'M WITH YOU ALL A HUNDRED PER CENT," said Harmon Shaver. "This is the most encouraging experience I've had in pictures." He had a bright bond salesman's chuckle. "By God, it reminds me of a circus we got up when I was a boy."

They had come to his office inconspicuously like conspirators – Jeff Manfred, Waggoner, Miss Starheim and Pat Hobby.

"You like the idea, Miss Starheim?" Shaver continued.

"I think it's wonderful."

"And you, Mr Waggoner?"

"I've heard only the general line," said Waggoner with director's caution, "but it seems to have the old emotional socko." He winked at Pat. "I didn't know this old tramp had it in him."

Pat glowed with pride. Jeff Manfred, though he was elated, was less sanguine.

"It's important nobody talks," he said nervously. "The Big Boys would find some way of killing it. In a week, when we've got the script done we'll go to them."

"I agree," said Shaver. "They have run the studio so long that, well, I don't trust my own secretaries – I sent them to the races this afternoon."

Back in Pat's office Eric, the call boy, was waiting. He did not know that he was the hinge upon which swung a great affair.

"You like the stuff, eh?" he asked eagerly.

"Pretty good," said Pat with calculated indifference.

"You said you'd pay more for the next batch."

"Have a heart!" Pat was aggrieved. "How many call boys get seventy-five a week?"

"How many call boys can write?"

Pat considered. Out of the two hundred a week Jeff Manfred was advancing from his own pocket, he had naturally awarded himself a commission of sixty per cent.

"I'll make it a hundred," he said. "Now check yourself off the lot and meet me in front of Benny's bar."

At the hospital, Estelle Hobby Devlin sat up in bed, overwhelmed by the unexpected visit.

"I'm glad you came, Pat," she said, "you've been very kind. Did you get my note?"

"Forget it," Pat said gruffly. He had never liked this wife. She had loved him too much – until she found suddenly that he was a poor lover. In her presence he felt inferior.

"I got a guy outside," he said.

"What for?"

"I thought maybe you had nothing to do and you might want to pay me back for all this jack…"

He waved his hand around the bare hospital room.

"You were a swell script girl once. Do you think if I got a typewriter you could put some good stuff into continuity?"

"Why – yes. I suppose I could."

"It's a secret. We can't trust anybody at the studio."

"All right," she said.

"I'll send this kid in with the stuff. I got a conference."

"All right… and – oh Pat – come and see me again."

"Sure, I'll come."

But he knew he wouldn't. He didn't like sickrooms – he lived in one himself. From now on he was done with poverty and failure. He admired strength – he was taking Lizzette Starheim to a wrestling match that night.

4

I N HIS PRIVATE MUSINGS Harmon Shaver referred to the showdown as "the surprise party". He was going to confront Le Vigne with a fait accompli, and he gathered his coterie before phoning Le Vigne to come over to his office.

"What for?" demanded Le Vigne. "Couldn't you tell me now – I'm busy as hell."

This arrogance irritated Shaver – who was here to watch over the interest of Eastern stockholders.

"I don't ask much," he said sharply. "I let you fellows laugh at me behind my back and freeze me out of things. But now I've got something and I'd like you to come over."

"All right – all right."

Le Vigne's eyebrows lifted as he saw the members of the new production unit, but he said nothing, sprawled into an armchair with his eyes on the floor and his fingers over his mouth.

Mr Shaver came around the desk and poured forth words that had been fermenting in him for months. Simmered to its essentials, his protest was: "You would not let me play, but I'm going to play anyhow." Then he nodded to Jeff Manfred – who opened the script and read aloud. This took an hour, and still Le Vigne sat motionless and silent.

"There you are," said Shaver triumphantly. "Unless you've got any objection, I think we ought to assign a budget to this proposition and get going. I'll answer to my people."

Le Vigne spoke at last.

"You like it, Miss Starheim?"

"I think it's wonderful."

"What language you going to play it in?"

To everyone's surprise Miss Starheim got to her feet.

"I must go now," she said with her faint poignant accent.

"Sit down and answer me," said Le Vigne. "What language are you playing it in?"

Miss Starheim looked tearful.

"Wenn I gute teachers hätte, könnte ich dann thees role gut spielen," she faltered.

"But you like the script."

She hesitated.

"I think it's wonderful."

Le Vigne turned to the others.

"Miss Starheim has been here eight months," he said. "She's had three teachers. Unless things have changed in the past two weeks, she can say just three sentences. She can say 'How do you do?'; she can say 'I think it's wonderful'; and she can say 'I must go now'. Miss Starheim has turned out to be a pinhead – I'm not insulting her, because she doesn't know what it means. Anyhow – there's your star."

He turned to Dutch Waggoner, but Dutch was already on his feet.

"Now Carl—" he said defensively.

"You force me to it," said Le Vigne. "I've trusted drunks up to a point, but I'll be goddamn if I'll trust a hophead."

He turned to Harmon Shaver.

"Dutch has been good for exactly one week apiece on his last four pictures. He's all right now, but as soon as the heat goes on he reaches for the little white powders. Now Dutch! Don't say anything you'll regret. We're carrying you in *hopes* – but you won't get on a stage till we've had a doctor's certificate for a year."

Again he turned to Harmon.

"There's your director. Your supervisor, Jeff Manfred, is here for one reason only – because he's Behrer's wife's cousin. There's nothing against him, but he belongs to silent days as much as… as much as…" – his eyes fell upon a quavering broken man – "as much as Pat Hobby."

"What do you mean?" demanded Jeff.

"You trusted Hobby, didn't you? That tells the whole story." He turned back to Shaver. "Jeff's a weeper and a wisher and a dreamer. Mr Shaver, you have bought a lot of condemned building material."

"Well, I've bought a good story," said Shaver defiantly.

"Yes. That's right. We'll make that story."

"Isn't that something?" demanded Shaver. "With all this secrecy, how was I to know about Mr Waggoner and Miss Starheim? But I do know a good story."

"Yes," said Le Vigne absently. He got up. "Yes – it's a good story… Come along to my office, Pat."

He was already at the door. Pat cast an agonized look at Mr Shaver as if for support. Then, weakly, he followed.

"Sit down, Pat."

"That Eric's got talent, hasn't he?" said Le Vigne. "He'll go places. How'd you come to dig him up?"

Pat felt the straps of the electric chair being adjusted.

"Oh – I just dug him up. He… came in my office."

"We're putting him on salary," said Le Vigne. "We ought to have some system to give these kids a chance."

He took a call on his Dictograph, then swung back to Pat.

"But how did you ever get mixed up with this goddam Shaver. *You*, Pat – an old-timer like you."

"Well, I thought—"

"Why doesn't he go back East?" continued Le Vigne disgustedly. "Getting all you poops stirred up!"

Blood flowed back into Pat's veins. He recognized his signal, his dog call.

"Well, I got you a story, didn't I?" he said, with almost a swagger. And he added, "How'd you know about it?"

"I went down to see Estelle in the hospital. She and this kid were working on it. I walked right in on them."

"Oh," said Pat.

"I knew the kid by sight. Now, Pat, tell me this: did Jeff Manfred think you wrote it – or was he in on the racket?"

"Oh God," Pat mourned. "What do I have to answer that for?"

Le Vigne leant forward intensely.

"Pat, you're sitting over a trapdoor!" he said with savage eyes. "Do you see how the carpet's cut? I just have to press this button and drop you down to hell! Will you *talk*?"

Pat was on his feet, staring wildly at the floor.

"Sure I will!" he cried. He believed it – he believed such things.

"All right," said Le Vigne relaxing. "There's whiskey in the sideboard there. Talk quick and I'll give you another month at two fifty. I kinda like having you around."

A Patriotic Short

PAT HOBBY, THE WRITER AND THE MAN, had his great success in Hollywood during what Irvin Cobb* refers to as "the mosaic-swimming-pool age – just before the era when they had to have a shinbone of St Sebastian for a clutch lever".

Mr Cobb no doubt exaggerates, for when Pat had his pool in those fat days of silent pictures, it was entirely cement, unless you should count the cracks where the water stubbornly sought its own level through the mud.

"But it *was* a pool," he assured himself one afternoon more than a decade later. Though he was now more than grateful for this small chore he had assigned him by producer Berners – one week at two fifty – all the insolence of office could not take that memory away.

He had been called in to the studio to work upon an humble short. It was based on the career of General Fitzhugh Lee who fought for the Confederacy and later for the USA against Spain – so it would offend neither North nor South. And in the recent conference Pat had tried to cooperate.

"I was thinking…" he suggested to Jack Berners, "that it might be a good thing if we could give it a Jewish touch."

"What do you mean?" demanded Jack Berners quickly.

"Well I thought – the way things are and all, it would be a sort of good thing to show that there were a number of Jews in it too."

"In what?"

"In the Civil War." Quickly he reviewed his meagre history. "They were, weren't they?"

"Naturally," said Berners, with some impatience, "I suppose everybody was, except the Quakers."

"Well, my idea was that we could have this Fitzhugh Lee in love with a Jewish girl. He's going to be shot at curfew, so she grabs a church bell—"

Jack Berners leant forward earnestly.

"Say, Pat, you want this job, don't you? Well, I told you the story. You got the first script. If you thought up this tripe to please me, you're losing your grip."

Was that a way to treat a man who had once owned a pool which had been talked about by...

That was how he happened to be thinking about his long-lost swimming pool as he entered the shorts department. He was remembering a certain day over a decade ago in all its details, how he had arrived at the studio in his car driven by a Filipino in uniform; the deferential bow of the guard at the gate which had admitted car and all to the lot, his ascent to that long-lost office which had a room for the secretary and was really a director's office...

His reverie was broken off by the voice of Ben Brown, head of the shorts department, who walked him into his own chambers.

"Jack Berners just phoned me," he said. "We don't want any new angles, Pat. We've got a good story. Fitzhugh Lee was a dashing cavalry commander. He was a nephew of Robert E. Lee and we want to show him at Appomattox, pretty bitter and all that. And then show how he became reconciled – we'll have to be careful because Virginia is swarming with Lees – and how he finally accepts a US commission from President McKinley…"

Pat's mind darted back again into the past. The President – that was the magic word that had gone around that morning many years ago. The President of the United States was going to make a visit to the lot. Everyone had been agog about it – it seemed to mark a new era in pictures because a President of the United States had never visited a studio before. The executives of the company were all dressed up – from a window of his long-lost Beverly Hills house Pat had seen Mr Maranda, whose mansion was next door to him, bustle down his walk in a cutaway coat at nine o'clock, and had known that something was up. He thought maybe it was clergy, but when he reached the lot he had found it was the President of the United States himself who was coming…

"Clean up the stuff about Spain," Ben Brown was saying. "The guy that wrote it was a Red, and he's got all the Spanish officers with ants in their pants. Fix up that."

In the office assigned him, Pat looked at the script of *True to Two Flags*. The first scene showed General Fitzhugh Lee at the head of his cavalry receiving word that Petersburg had been evacuated. In the script Lee took the blow in pantomime, but Pat was getting two fifty a week – so, casually and without effort, he wrote in one of his favourite lines:

Lee (to his officers)
Well, what are you standing here gawking for? DO *something!*
6. Medium Shot Officers pepping up, slapping each other on back, etc.
Dissolve to:

To what? Pat's mind dissolved once more into the glamorous past. On that happy day in the Twenties his phone had rung at about noon. It had been Mr Maranda.

"Pat, the President is lunching in the private dining room. Doug Fairbanks can't come so there's a place empty and anyhow we think there ought to be one writer there."

His memory of the luncheon was palpitant with glamour. The Great Man had asked some questions about pictures and had told a joke and Pat had laughed and laughed with the others – all of them solid men together – rich, happy and successful.

Afterwards the President was to go on some sets and see some scenes taken, and still later he was going to Mr Maranda's house to meet some of the women stars at tea. Pat was not invited to that party, but he went home early anyhow and from his veranda saw the cortège drive up, with Mr Maranda beside the President in the back seat. Ah he was proud of pictures then – of his position in them – of the President of the happy country where he was born...

Returning to reality, Pat looked down at the script of *True to Two Flags* and wrote slowly and thoughtfully:

Insert: A calendar – with the years plainly marked and the sheets blowing off in a cold wind, to show Fitzhugh Lee growing older and older.

His labours had made him thirsty – not for water, but he knew better than to take anything else his first day on the job. He got up and went out into the hall and along the corridor to the water cooler.

As he walked, he slipped back into his reverie.

That had been a lovely California afternoon, so Mr Maranda had taken his exalted guest and the coterie of stars into his garden, which adjoined Pat's garden. Pat had gone out his back door and followed a low privet hedge keeping out of sight – and then accidentally come face to face with the Presidential party.

The President had smiled and nodded. Mr Maranda smiled and nodded.

"You met Mr Hobby at lunch," Mr Maranda said to the President. "He's one of our writers."

"Oh yes," said the President, "you write the pictures."

"Yes I do," said Pat.

The President glanced over into Pat's property.

"I suppose," he said, "that you get lots of inspiration sitting by the side of that fine pool."

"Yes," said Pat, "yes, I do."

…Pat filled his cup at the cooler. Down the hall there was a group approaching – Jack Berners, Ben Brown and several other executives, and with them a girl to whom they were very attentive and deferential. He recognized her face – she was the girl of the year, the It girl, the Oomph girl, the Glamour Girl, the girl for whose services every studio was in violent competition.

Pat lingered over his drink. He had seen many phoneys break in and break out again, but this girl was the real thing, someone to stir every pulse in the nation. He felt his own heart beat faster. Finally, as the procession drew near, he put down the cup, dabbed at his hair with his hand and took a step out into the corridor.

The girl looked at him – he looked at the girl. Then she took one arm of Jack Berners's and one of Ben Brown's and suddenly the party seemed to walk right through him – so that he had to take a step back against the wall.

An instant later, Jack Berners turned around and said back to him, "Hello, Pat." And then some of the others threw half-glances around but no one else spoke, so interested were they in the girl.

In his office, Pat looked at the scene where President McKinley offers a United States commission to Fitzhugh Lee. Suddenly he gritted his teeth and bore down on his pencil as he wrote:

Lee
Mr President, you can take your commission and go straight to hell.

Then he bent down over his desk, his shoulders shaking as he thought of that happy day when he had had a swimming pool.

On the Trail of Pat Hobby

1

T HE DAY WAS DARK from the outset, and a California fog crept everywhere. It had followed Pat in his headlong, hatless flight across the city. His destination, his refuge, was the studio, where he was not employed, but which had been home to him for twenty years.

Was it his imagination or did the policeman at the gate give him and his pass an especially long look? It might be the lack of a hat – Hollywood was full of hatless men, but Pat felt marked, especially as there had been no opportunity to part his thin grey hair.

In the writers' building he went into the lavatory. Then he remembered: by some inspired ukase from above, all mirrors had been removed from the writers' building a year ago.

Across the hall he saw Bee McIlvaine's door ajar, and discerned her plump person.

"Bee, can you loan me your compact box?" he asked.

Bee looked at him suspiciously, then frowned and dug it from her purse.

"You on the lot?" she enquired.

"Will be next week," he prophesied. He put the compact on her desk and bent over it with his comb. "Why won't they put mirrors back in the johnnies? Do they think writers would look at themselves all day?"

"Remember when they took out the couches?" said Bee. "In nineteen thirty-two. And they put them back in thirty-four."

"I worked at home," said Pat feelingly.

Finished with her mirror, he wondered if she were good for a loan – enough to buy a hat and something to eat. Bee must have seen the look in his eyes, for she forestalled him.

"The Finns got all my money," she said, "and I'm worried about my job. Either my picture starts tomorrow or it's going to be shelved. We haven't even got a title."

She handled him a mimeographed bulletin from the scenario department, and Pat glanced at the headline.

TO ALL DEPARTMENTS

TITLE WANTED — FIFTY DOLLARS REWARD

SUMMARY FOLLOWS

"I could use fifty," Pat said. "What's it about?"

"It's written there. It's about a lot of stuff that goes on in tourist cabins."

Pat started and looked at her wild-eyed. He had thought to be safe here behind the guarded gates, but news travelled fast. This was a friendly or perhaps not so friendly warning. He must move on. He was a hunted man now, with nowhere to lay his hatless head.

"I don't know anything about that," he mumbled and walked hastily from the room.

2

J UST INSIDE THE DOOR of the commissary, Pat looked around. There was no guardian except the girl at the cigarette stand, but obtaining another person's hat was subject to one complication: it was hard to judge the size by a cursory glance, while the sight of a man trying on several hats in a check room was unavoidably suspicious.

Personal taste also obtruded itself. Pat was beguiled by a green fedora with a sprightly feather, but it was too readily identifiable. This was also true of a fine white Stetson for the open spaces. Finally he decided on a sturdy grey Homburg, which looked as if it would give him good service. With trembling hands he put it on. It fitted. He walked out – in painful, interminable slow motion.

His confidence was partly restored in the next hour by the fact that no one he encountered made references to tourists' cabins. It had been a lean three months for Pat. He had regarded his job as night clerk for the Selecto Tourists Cabins as a mere fill-in, never to be mentioned to his friends. But when the police squad came this morning they held up the raid long enough to assure Pat, or Don Smith as he called himself, that he would be wanted as a witness. The story of his escape lies in the realm of melodrama, how he went out a side door, bought a half-pint of what he so desperately needed at the corner drugstore, hitch-hiked his way across the great city, going limp at the sight of traffic cops and only breathing free when he saw the studio's high-flown sign.

After a call on Louie, the studio bookie, whose great patron he once had been, he dropped in on Jack Berners. He had no idea to submit, but he caught Jack in a hurried moment flying off to a producers' conference and was unexpectedly invited to step in and wait for his return.

The office was rich and comfortable. There were no letters worth reading on the desk, but there were a decanter and glasses in a cupboard, and presently he lay down on a big soft couch and fell asleep.

He was awakened by Berners's return, in high indignation.

"Of all the damn nonsense! We get a hurry call – heads of all departments. One man is late and we wait for him. He comes in and gets a bawling-out for wasting thousands of dollars' worth of time. Then what do you suppose: Mr Marcus has lost his favourite hat!"

Pat failed to associate the fact with himself.

"All the department heads stop production!" continued Berners. "Two thousand people look for a grey Homburg hat!" He sank despairingly into a chair. "I can't talk to you today, Pat. By four o'clock I've got to get a title to a picture about a tourist camp. Got an idea?"

"No," said Pat. "No."

"Well, go up to Bee McIlvaine's office and help her figure something out. There's fifty dollars in it."

In a daze, Pat wandered to the door.

"Hey," said Berners, "don't forget your hat."

3

FEELING THE EFFECTS OF HIS DAY outside the law, and of a tumbler full of Berners's brandy, Pat sat in Bee McIlvaine's office.

"We've got to get a title," said Bee gloomily.

She handed Pat the mimeograph offering fifty dollars reward and put a pencil in his hand. Pat stared at the paper unseeingly.

"How about it?" she asked. "Who's got a title?"

There was a long silence.

"*Test Pilot*'s been used, hasn't it?" he said with a vague tone.

"Wake up! This isn't about aviation."

"Well, I was just thinking it was a good title."

"So's *The Birth of a Nation*."

"But not for this picture," Pat muttered. "*Birth of a Nation* wouldn't suit this picture."

"Are you ribbing me?" demanded Bee. "Or are you losing your mind? This is serious."

"Sure – I know." Feebly he scrawled words at the bottom of the page. "I've had a couple of drinks that's all. My head'll clear up in a minute. I'm trying to think what have been the most successful titles. The trouble is they've all been used, like *It Happened One Night*."

Bee looked at him uneasily. He was having trouble keeping his eyes open, and she did not want him to pass out in her office. After a minute she called Jack Berners.

"Could you possibly come up? I've got some title ideas."

Jack arrived with a sheaf of suggestions sent in from here and there in the studio, but digging through them yielded no ore.

"How about it, Pat? Got anything?"

Pat braced himself to an effort.

"I like *It Happened One Morning*," he said – then looked desperately at his scrawl on the mimeograph paper, "or else – *Grand Motel*."

Berners smiled.

"*Grand Motel*," he repeated. "By God! I think you've got something. *Grand Motel*."

"I said *Grand Hotel*," said Pat.

"No, you didn't. You said *Grand Motel* – and for my money it wins the fifty."

"I've got to go lie down," announced Pat. "I feel sick."

"There's an empty office across the way. That's a funny idea Pat, *Grand Motel* – or else *Motel Clerk*. How do you like that?"

As the fugitive quickened his step out the door, Bee pressed the hat into his hands.

"Good work, old-timer," she said.

Pat seized Mr Marcus's hat, and stood holding it there like a bowl of soup.

"Feel – better – now," he mumbled after a moment. "Be back for the money."

And carrying his burden he shambled towards the lavatory.

Fun in an Artist's Studio

1

THIS WAS BACK IN 1938, when few people except the Germans knew that they had already won their war in Europe. People still cared about art and tried to make it out of everything, from old clothes to orange peel, and that was how the Princess Dignanni found Pat. She wanted to make art out of him.

"No, not you, Mr DeTinc," she said. "I can't paint you. You are a very standardized product, Mr DeTinc."

Mr DeTinc, who was a power in pictures and had even been photographed with Mr Duchman, the Secret Sin specialist, stepped smoothly out of the way. He was not offended – in his whole life Mr DeTinc had never been offended – but especially not now, for the Princess did not want to paint Clark Gable or Spencer Rooney or Vivien Leigh either.

She saw Pat in the commissary and found he was a writer, and asked that he be invited to Mr DeTinc's party. The Princess was a pretty woman born in Boston, Massachusetts, and Pat was forty-nine with red-rimmed eyes and a soft purr of whiskey on his breath.

"You write scenarios, Mr Hobby?"

"I help," said Pat. "Takes more than one person to prepare a script."

He was flattered by this attention and not a little suspicious. It was only because his supervisor was a nervous wreck that he happened to have a job at all. His supervisor had forgotten a week ago that he had hired Pat, and when Pat was spotted in the commissary and told he was wanted at Mr DeTinc's house, the writer had passed a *mauvais quart d'heure*.* It did not even look like the kind of party that Pat had known in his prosperous days. There was not so much as a drunk passed out in the downstairs toilet.

"I imagine scenario-writing is very well paid," said the Princess.

Pat glanced around to see who was within hearing. Mr DeTinc had withdrawn his huge bulk somewhat, but one of his apparently independent eyes seemed fixed glittering on Pat.

"Very well paid," said Pat – and he added in a lower voice: "if you can get it."

The Princess seemed to understand and lowered her voice too.

"You mean writers have trouble getting work?"

He nodded.

"Too many of 'em get in these unions." He raised his voice a little for Mr DeTinc's benefit. "They're all Reds, most of these writers."

The Princess nodded.

"Will you turn your face a little to the light?" she said politely. "There, that's fine. You won't mind coming to my studio tomorrow, will you? Just to pose for me an hour?"

He scrutinized her again.

"Naked?" he asked cautiously.

"Oh, no," she averred. "Just the head."

Mr DeTinc moved nearer and nodded.

"You ought to go. Princess Dignanni is going to paint some of the biggest stars here. Going to paint Jack Benny and Baby Sandy and Hedy Lamarr* – isn't that a fact, Princess?"

The artist didn't answer. She was a pretty good portrait painter and she knew just how good she was and just how much of it was her title. She was hesitating between her several manners – Picasso's rose period with a flash of Boldini, or straight Reginald Marsh.* But she knew what she was going to call it. She was going to call it *Hollywood and Vine*.

2

I N SPITE OF THE REASSURANCE that he would be clothed, Pat approached the rendezvous with uneasiness. In his young and impressionable years he had looked through a peephole into a machine where two dozen postcards slapped before his eyes in sequence. The story unfolded was *Fun in an Artist's Studio*. Even now with the striptease a legalized municipal project, he was a little shocked at the remembrance, and when he presented himself next day at the Princess's bungalow at the Beverly Hills Hotel it would not have surprised him if she had met him in a Turkish towel. He was disappointed. She wore a smock and her black hair was brushed straight back like a boy's.

Pat had stopped off for a couple of drinks on the way, but his first words: "How'ya Duchess?" failed to set a jovial note for the occasion.

"Well, Mr Hobby," she said coolly, "it's nice of you to spare me an afternoon."

"We don't work too hard in Hollywood," he assured her. "Everything is *mañana* – in Spanish that means tomorrow."

She led him forthwith into a rear apartment, where an easel stood on a square of canvas by the window. There was a couch and they sat down.

"I want to get used to you for a minute," she said. "Did you ever pose before?"

"Do I look that way?" He winked, and when she smiled he felt better and asked: "You haven't got a drink around, have you?"

The Princess hesitated. She had wanted him to look as if he *needed* one. Compromising, she went to the icebox and fixed him a small highball. She returned to find that he had taken off his coat and tie and lay informally upon the couch.

"That *is* better," the Princess said. "That shirt you're wearing. I think they make them for Hollywood – like the special prints they make for Ceylon and Guatemala. Now drink this and we'll get to work."

"Why don't you have a drink too and make it friendly?" Pat suggested.

"I had one in the pantry," she lied.

"Married woman?" he asked.

"I have been married. Now would you mind sitting on this stool?"

Reluctantly Pat got up, took down the highball, somewhat thwarted by the thin taste, and moved to the stool. "Now sit very still," she said.

He sat silent as she worked. It was three o'clock. They were running the third race at Santa Anita and he had ten bucks on the nose. That made sixty he owed Louie, the studio bookie, and Louie stood determinedly beside him at the pay window every Thursday.

This dame had good legs under the easel – her red lips pleased him and the way her bare arms moved as she worked. Once upon a time he wouldn't have looked at a woman over twenty-five, unless it was a secretary right in the office with him. But the kids you saw around now were snooty – always talking about calling the police.

"Please sit still, Mr Hobby."

"What say we knock off," he suggested. "This work makes you thirsty."

The Princess had been painting half an hour. Now she stopped and stared at him a moment.

"Mr Hobby, you were loaned me by Mr DeTinc. Why don't you act just as if you were working over at the studio? I'll be through in another half-hour."

"What do I get out of it?" he demanded. "I'm no poser – I'm a writer."

"Your studio salary has not stopped," she said, resuming her work. "What does it matter if Mr DeTinc wants you to do this?"

"It's different. You're a dame. I've got my self-respect to think of."

"What do you expect me to do – flirt with you?"

"No – that's old stuff. But I thought we could sit around and have a drink."

"Perhaps later," she said, and then: "Is this harder work than the studio? Am I so difficult to look at?"

"I don't mind looking at you, but why couldn't we sit on the sofa?"

"You don't sit on the sofa at the studio."

"Sure you do. Listen, if you tried all the doors in the Writers' Building you'd find a lot of them locked, and don't you forget it."

She stepped back and squinted at him.

"Locked? To be undisturbed?" She put down her brush. "I'll get you a drink."

When she returned, she stopped for a moment in the doorway – Pat had removed his shirt and stood rather sheepishly in the middle of the floor holding it towards her.

"Here's that shirt," he said. "You can have it. I know where I can get a lot more."

For a moment longer she regarded him; then she took the shirt and put it on the sofa.

"Sit down and let me finish," she said. As he hesitated, she added, "Then we'll have a drink together."

"When'll that be?"

"Fifteen minutes."

She worked quickly – several times she was content with the lower face – several times she deliberated and started over. Something that she had seen in the commissary was missing.

"Been an artist a long time?" Pat asked.

"Many years."

"Been around artists' studios a lot?"

"Quite a lot – I've had my own studios."

"I guess a lot goes on around those studios. Did you ever..."
He hesitated.

"Ever what?" she queried.

"Did you ever paint a naked man?"

"Don't talk for one minute, please." She paused with brush uplifted, seemed to listen, then made a swift stroke and looked doubtfully at the result.

"Do you know you're difficult to paint?" she said, laying down the brush.

"I don't like this posing around," he admitted. "Let's call it a day." He stood up. "Why don't you – why don't you slip into something so you'll be comfortable?"

The Princess smiled. She would tell her friends this story – it would sort of go with the picture, if the picture was any good, which she now doubted.

"You ought to revise your methods," she said. "Do you have much success with this approach?"

Pat lit a cigarette and sat down.

"If you were eighteen, see, I'd give you that line about being nuts about you."

"But why any line at all?"

"Oh, come off it!" he advised her. "You wanted to paint me, didn't you?"

"Yes."

"Well, when a dame wants to paint a guy..." Pat reached down and undid his shoe strings, kicked his shoes onto the floor, put his stockinged feet on the couch. "...when a dame wants to see a guy about something or a guy wants to see a dame, there's a pay-off, see."

The Princess sighed. "Well I seem to be trapped," she said. "But it makes it rather difficult when a dame just wants to paint a guy."

"When a dame wants to paint a guy..." Pat half-closed his eyes, nodded and flapped his hands expressively. As his thumbs went suddenly towards his suspenders, she spoke in a louder voice.

"Officer!"

There was a sound behind Pat. He turned to see a young man in khaki with shining black gloves, standing in the door.

"Officer, this man is an employee of Mr DeTinc's. Mr DeTinc lent him to me for the afternoon."

The policeman looked at the staring image of guilt upon the couch.

"Get fresh?" he enquired.

"I don't want to prefer charges – I called the desk to be on the safe side. He was to pose for me in the nude and now he refuses." She walked casually to her easel. "Mr Hobby, why don't you stop this mock modesty – you'll find a Turkish towel in the bathroom."

Pat reached stupidly for his shoes. Somehow it flashed into his mind that they were running the eighth race at Santa Anita…

"Shake it up, you," said the cop. "You heard what the lady said."

Pat stood up vaguely and fixed a long poignant look on the Princess.

"You told me…" he said hoarsely, "you wanted to paint—"

"You told me I meant something else. Hurry please. And officer, there's a drink in the pantry."

…A few minutes later, as Pat sat shivering in the centre of the room, his memory went back to those peep shows of his youth – though at the moment he could see little resemblance. He was grateful at least for the Turkish towel, even now failing to realize that the Princess was not interested in his shattered frame but in his face.

It wore the exact expression that had wooed her in the commissary, the expression of Hollywood and Vine, the other self of Mr DeTinc – and she worked fast while there was still light enough to paint by.

Two Old-Timers

PHIL MACEDON, once the Star of Stars, and Pat Hobby, scriptwriter, had collided out on Sunset near the Beverly Hills Hotel. It was five in the morning and there was liquor in the air as they argued, and Sergeant Gaspar took them around to the station house. Pat Hobby, a man of forty- nine, showed fight, apparently because Phil Macedon failed to acknowledge that they were old acquaintances.

He accidentally bumped Sergeant Gaspar, who was so provoked that he put him in a little barred room while they waited for the captain to arrive.

Chronologically Phil Macedon belonged between Eugene O'Brien and Robert Taylor.* He was still a handsome man in his early fifties and he had saved enough from his great days for a hacienda in the San Fernando Valley; there he rested as full of honours, as rollick-some and with the same purposes in life as Man o' War.*

With Pat Hobby life had dealt otherwise. After twenty-one years in the industry, script and publicity, the accident found him driving a 1933 car which had lately become the property of the North Hollywood Finance and Loan Co. And once, back in 1928, he had reached a point of getting bids for a private swimming pool.

He glowered from his confinement, still resenting Macedon's failure to acknowledge that they had ever met before.

"I suppose you don't remember Colman," he said sarcastically. "Or Connie Talmadge or Bill Corker or Allan Dwan."*

Macedon lit a cigarette with the sort of timing in which the silent screen has never been surpassed, and offered one to Sergeant Gaspar.

"Couldn't I come in tomorrow?" he asked. "I have a horse to exercise…"

"I'm sorry, Mr Macedon," said the cop – sincerely, for the actor was an old favourite of his. "The Captain is due here any minute. After that we won't be holding *you*."

"It's just a formality," said Pat, from his cell.

"Yeah, it's just a…" Sergeant Gaspar glared at Pat. "It may not be any formality for *you*. Did you ever hear of the sobriety test?"

Macedon flicked his cigarette out the door and lit another.

"Suppose I come back in a couple of hours," he suggested.

"No," regretted Sergeant Gaspar. "And since I have to detain you, Mr Macedon, I want to take the opportunity to tell you what you meant to me once. It was that picture you made. *The Final Push*, it meant a lot to every man who was in the war."

"Oh, yes," said Macedon, smiling.

"I used to try to tell my wife about the war – how it was, with the shells and the machine guns – I was in there seven months with the 26th New England – but she never understood. She'd point her finger at me and say, 'Boom! you're dead,' and so I'd laugh and stop trying to make her understand."

"Hey, can I get out of here?" demanded Pat.

"You shut up!" said Gaspar fiercely. "You probably wasn't in the war."

"I was in the Motion Picture Home Guard," said Pat. "I had bad eyes."

"Listen to him," said Gaspar disgustedly. "That's what all them slackers say. Well, the war was something. And after my wife saw that picture of yours I never had to explain to her. She knew. She always spoke different about it after that – never just pointed her finger at me and said 'Boom!' I'll never forget the part where you was in that shell hole. That was so real it made my hands sweat."

"Thanks," said Macedon graciously. He lit another cigarette, "You see, I was in the war myself and I knew how it was. I knew how it felt."

"Yes, sir," said Gaspar appreciatively. "Well, I'm glad of the opportunity to tell you what you did for me. You… you explained the war to my wife."

"What are you talking about?" demanded Pat Hobby suddenly. "That war picture Bill Corker did in 1925?"

"There he goes again," said Gaspar. "Sure – *The Birth of a Nation*. Now you pipe down till the Captain comes."

"Phil Macedon knew me then all right," said Pat resentfully. "I even watched him work on it one day."

"I just don't happen to remember you, old man," said Macedon politely. "I can't help that."

"You remember the day Bill Corker shot that shell-hole sequence don't you? Your first day on the picture?"

There was a moment's silence.

"When will the Captain be here?" Macedon asked.

"Any minute now, Mr Macedon."

"Well, I remember," said Pat, "because I was there when he had that shell hole dug. He was out there on the back lot at nine o'clock in the morning with a gang of hunkies to dig the hole and four cameras. He called you up from a field telephone and told you to go to the costumer and get into a soldier suit. Now you remember?"

"I don't load my mind with details, old man."

"You called up that they didn't have one to fit you, and Corker told you to shut up and get into one anyhow. When you got out to the back lot you were sore as hell because your suit didn't fit."

Macedon smiled charmingly.

"You have a most remarkable memory. Are you sure you have the right picture – and the right actor?" he asked.

"Am I!" said Pat grimly. "I can see you right now. Only you didn't have much time to complain about the uniform, because that wasn't Corker's plan. He always thought you were the toughest ham in Hollywood to get anything natural out of – and he had a scheme. He was going to get the heart of the picture shot by noon – before you even knew you were acting. He turned you around and shoved you down into that shell hole on your fanny, and yelled, 'Camera.'"

"That's a lie," said Phil Macedon. "I *got* down."

"Then why did you start yelling?" demanded Pat. "I can still hear you: 'Hey, what's the idea? Is this some… gag? You get me out of here or I'll walk out on you!' And all the time you were trying to claw your way up the side of that pit, so damn mad you couldn't see. You'd almost get up and then you'd slide back and lie there with your face working – till finally you began to bawl, and all this time Bill had four cameras on you. After about twenty minutes you gave up and just lay there, heaving. Bill took a hundred feet of that and then he had a couple of prop men pull you out."

The Police Captain had arrived in the squad car. He stood in the doorway against the first grey of dawn.

"What you got here, Sergeant? A drunk?"

Sergeant Gaspar walked over to the cell, unlocked it and beckoned Pat to come out. Pat blinked a moment – then his eyes fell on Phil Macedon and he shook his finger at him.

"So you see, I *do* know you," he said. "Bill Corker cut that piece of film and titled it so you were supposed to be a doughboy whose pal had just been killed. You wanted to climb out and get at the Germans in revenge, but the shells bursting all around and the concussions kept knocking you back in."

"What's it about?" demanded the Captain.

"I want to prove I know this guy," said Pat. "Bill said the best moment in the picture was when Phil was yelling, 'I've al*ready* broken my first fingernail!' Bill titled it 'Ten Huns will go to hell to shine your shoes!'"

"You've got here 'collision with alcohol'," said the Captain, looking at the blotter. "Let's take these guys down to the hospital and give them the test."

"Look here now," said the actor, with his flashing smile, "my name's Phil Macedon."

The Captain was a political appointee and very young. He remembered the name and the face, but he was not especially impressed, because Hollywood was full of has-beens.

They all got into the squad car at the door.

After the test, Macedon was held at the station house until friends could arrange bail. Pat Hobby was discharged, but his car would not run, so Sergeant Gaspar offered to drive him home.

"Where do you live?" he asked as they started off.

"I don't live anywhere tonight," said Pat. "That's why I was driving around. When a friend of mine wakes up I'll touch him for a couple of bucks and go to a hotel."

"Well now," said Sergeant Gaspar, "I got a couple of bucks that ain't working."

The great mansions of Beverly Hills slid by and Pat waved his hand at them in salute.

"In the good old days," he said, "I used to be able to drop in to some of those houses day or night. And Sunday mornings—"

"Is that all true you said in the station," Gaspar asked, "about how they put him in the hole?"

"Sure, it is," said Pat. "That guy needn't have been so upstage. He's just an old-timer like me."

Mightier than the Sword

1

THE SWARTHY MAN, with eyes that snapped back and forward on a rubber band from the rear of his head, answered to the alias of Dick Dale. The tall, spectacled man who was put together like a camel without a hump – and you missed the hump – answered to the name of E. Brunswick Hudson. The scene was a shoeshine stand, insignificant unit of the great studio. We perceive it through the red-rimmed eyes of Pat Hobby who sat in the chair beside Director Dale.

The stand was out of doors, opposite the commissary. The voice of E. Brunswick Hudson quivered with passion, but it was pitched low so as not to reach passers-by.

"I don't know what a writer like me is doing out here anyhow," he said, with vibrations.

Pat Hobby, who was an old-timer, could have supplied the answer, but he had not the acquaintance of the other two.

"It's a funny business," said Dick Dale, and to the shoeshine boy. "Use that saddle soap."

"Funny!" thundered E. "It's *sus*pect! Here, against my better judgement, I write just what you tell me – and the office tells me to get out because we can't seem to agree."

"That's polite," explained Dick Dale. "What do you want me to do – knock you down?"

E. Brunswick Hudson removed his glasses.

"Try it!" he suggested. "I weigh a hundred and sixty-two and I haven't got an ounce of flesh on me." He hesitated and redeemed himself from this extremity. "I mean *fat* on me."

"Oh, to hell with that!" said Dick Dale contemptuously. "I can't mix it up with you. I got to figure this picture. You go back East and write one of your books and forget it." Momentarily he looked at Pat Hobby, smiling as if *he* would understand, as if anyone would understand except E. Brunswick Hudson. "I can't tell you all about pictures in three weeks."

Hudson replaced his spectacles.

"When I *do* write a book," he said, "I'll make you the laughing-stock of the nation."

He withdrew, ineffectual, baffled, defeated. After a minute, Pat spoke.

"Those guys can never get the idea," he commented. "I've never seen one get the idea and I been in this business, publicity and script, for twenty years."

"You on the lot?" Dale asked.

Pat hesitated.

"Just finished a job," he said.

That was five months before.

"What screen credits you got?" Dale asked.

"I got credits going all the way back to 1920."

"Come up to my office," Dick Dale said. "I got something I'd like to talk over – now that bastard is gone back to his New England farm. Why do they have to get a New England farm – with the whole West not settled?"

Pat gave his second-to-last dime to the bootblack and climbed down from the stand.

2

WE ARE IN THE MIDST of technicalities.

"The trouble is this composer Reginald de Koven* didn't have any colour," said Dick Dale. "He wasn't deaf like Beethoven or a singing waiter or get put in jail or anything. All he did was write music and all we got for an angle is that song 'O Promise Me'. We got to weave something around that – a dame promises him something and in the end he collects."

"I want time to think it over in my mind," said Pat. "If Jack Berners will put me on the picture—"

"He'll put you on," said Dick Dale. "From now on I'm picking my own writers. What do you get – fifteen hundred?" He looked at Pat's shoes. "Seven fifty?"

Pat stared at him blankly for a moment; then out of thin air, produced his best piece of imaginative fiction in a decade.

"I was mixed up with a producer's wife," he said, "and they ganged up on me. I only get three fifty now."

In some ways it was the easiest job he had ever had. Director Dick Dale was a type that, fifty years ago, could be found in any American town. Generally he was the local photographer, usually he was the originator of small mechanical contrivances and a leader in bizarre local movements, almost always he contributed verse to the local press. All the most energetic embodiments of this "Sensation Type" had migrated to Hollywood between 1910 and 1930, and there they had achieved a psychological fulfilment inconceivable in any other time or place. At last, and on a large scale, they were able to have their way. In the weeks that Pat Hobby and Mabel Hatman, Mr Dale's script girl, sat beside him and worked on the script, not a movement, not a word went into it that was not Dick Dale's coinage. Pat would venture a suggestion, something that was "Always good".

"Wait a minute! Wait a minute!" Dick Dale was on his feet, his hands outspread. "I seem to see a dog." They would wait, tense and breathless, while he saw a dog.

"Two dogs."

A second dog took its place beside the first in their obedient visions.

"We open on a dog on a leash – pull the camera back to show another dog – now they're snapping at each other. We pull back further – the leashes are attached to tables – the tables tip over. See it?"

Or else, out of a clear sky.

"I seem to see De Koven as a plasterer's apprentice."

"Yes." This hopefully.

"He goes to Santa Anita and plasters the walls, singing at his work. Take that down, Mabel." He continued on…

In a month they had the requisite hundred and twenty pages. Reginald de Koven, it seemed, though not an alcoholic, was too fond of "the Little Brown Jug". The father of the girl he loved had died of drink, and after the wedding, when she found him drinking from the Little Brown Jug, nothing would do but that she should go away, for twenty years. He became famous and she sang his songs as Maid Marian, but he never knew it was the same girl.

The script, marked "Temporary Complete. From Pat Hobby", went up to the head office. The schedule called for Dale to begin shooting in a week.

Twenty-four hours later he sat with his staff in his office, in an atmosphere of blue gloom. Pat Hobby was the least depressed. Four weeks at three fifty, even allowing for the two hundred that had slipped away at Santa Anita, was a far cry from the twenty cents he had owned on the shoeshine stand.

"That's pictures, Dick," he said consolingly. "You're up – you're down – you're in, you're out. Any old-timer knows."

"Yes," said Dick Dale absently. "Mabel, phone that E. Brunswick Hudson. He's on his New England farm – maybe milking bees."

In a few minutes she reported.

"He flew into Hollywood this morning, Mr Dale. I've located him at the Beverly Wilshire Hotel."

Dick Dale pressed his ear to the phone. His voice was bland and friendly as he said:

"Mr Hudson, there was one day here you had an idea I liked. You said you were going to write it up. It was about this De Koven stealing his music from a sheep-herder up in Vermont. Remember?"

"Yes."

"Well, Berners wants to go into production right away, or else we can't have the cast, so we're on the spot, if you know what I mean. Do you happen to have that stuff?"

"You remember when I brought it to you?" Hudson asked. "You kept me waiting two hours – then you looked at it for two minutes. Your neck hurt you – I think it needed wringing. God, how it hurt you. That was the only nice thing about that morning."

"In picture business—"

"I'm so glad you're stuck. I wouldn't tell you the story of *The Three Bears* for fifty grand."

As the phones clicked, Dick Dale turned to Pat.

"Goddamn writers!" he said savagely. "What do we pay you for? Millions – and you write a lot of tripe I can't photograph and get sore if we don't read your lousy stuff! How can a man make pictures when they give me two bastards like you and Hudson. How? How do you think – you old whiskey bum!"

Pat rose – took a step towards the door. He didn't know, he said.

"Get out of here!" cried Dick Dale. "You're off the payroll. Get off the lot."

Fate had not dealt Pat a farm in New England, but there was a café just across from the studio where bucolic dreams blossomed in bottles if you had the money. He did not like to leave the lot, which for many years had been home for him, so he came back at six and went up to his office. It was locked. He saw that they had already allotted it to another writer – the name on the door was E. Brunswick Hudson.

He spent an hour in the commissary, made another visit to the bar, and then some instinct led him to a stage where there was a bedroom set. He passed the night upon a couch occupied by Claudette Colbert in the fluffiest ruffles only that afternoon.

Morning was bleaker, but he had a little in his bottle and almost a hundred dollars in his pocket. The horses were running at Santa Anita and he might double it by night.

On his way out of the lot, he hesitated beside the barber shop, but he felt too nervous for a shave. Then he paused, for from the direction of the shoeshine stand he heard Dick Dale's voice.

"Miss Hatman found your other script, and it happens to be the property of the company."

E. Brunswick Hudson stood at the foot of the stand.

"I won't have my name used," he said.

"That's good. I'll put her name on it. Berners thinks it's great, if the De Koven family will stand for it. Hell – the sheep-breeder never would have been able to market those tunes anyhow. Ever hear of any sheep-herder drawing down jack from ASCAP?"*

Hudson took off his spectacles.

"I weigh a hundred and sixty-three..."

Pat moved in closer.

"Join the army," said Dale contemptuously. "I got no time for mixing it up. I got to make a picture." His eyes fell on Pat. "Hello, old-timer."

"Hello, Dick," said Pat, smiling. Then, knowing the advantage of the psychological moment, he took his chance.

"When do we work?" he said.

"How much?" Dick Dale asked the shoeshine boy – and to Pat: "It's all done. I promised Mabel a screen credit for a long time. Look me up some day when you got an idea."

He hailed someone by the barber shop and hurried off. Hudson and Hobby, men of letters who had never met, regarded each other. There were tears of anger in Hudson's eyes.

"Authors get a tough break out here," Pat said sympathetically. "They never ought to come."

"Who'd make up the stories – these feebs?"

"Well anyhow, not authors," said Pat. "They don't want authors. They want writers – like me."

Pat Hobby's College Days

1

THE AFTERNOON WAS DARK. The walls of Topanga Canyon rose sheer on either side. Get rid of it she must. The clank-clank in the back seat frightened her. Evylyn did not like the business at all. It was not what she came out here to do. Then she thought of Mr Hobby. He believed in her, trusted her – and she was doing this for him.

But the mission was arduous. Evylyn Lascalles left the canyon and cruised along the inhospitable shores of Beverly Hills. Several times she turned up alleys, several times she parked beside vacant lots – but always some pedestrian or loiterer threw her into a mood of nervous anxiety. Once her heart almost stopped as she was eyed with appreciation – or was it suspicion – by a man who looked like a detective.

He had no right to ask me this, she said to herself. Never again. I'll tell him so. Never again.

Night was fast descending. Evylyn Lascalles had never seen it come down so fast. Back to the canyon then, to the wild, free life. She drove up a paint-box corridor which gave its last pastel shades to the day. And reached a certain security at a bend overlooking plateau land far below.

Here there could be no complication. As she threw each article over the cliff it would be as far removed from her as if she were in a different state of the Union.

Miss Lascalles was from Brooklyn. She had wanted very much to come to Hollywood and be a secretary in pictures – now she wished that she had never left her home.

On with the job though – she must part with her cargo – as soon as this next car passed the bend…

2

…MEANWHILE HER EMPLOYER, Pat Hobby, stood in front of the barber shop talking to Louie, the studio bookie. Pat's four weeks at two fifty would be up tomorrow, and he had begun to have that harassed and aghast feeling of those who live always on the edge of solvency.

"Four lousy weeks on a bad script," he said. "That's all I've had in six months."

"How do you live?" asked Louie – without *too* much show of interest.

"I don't live. The days go by, the weeks go by. But who cares? Who cares – after twenty years."

"You had a good time in your day," Louie reminded him.

Pat looked after a dress extra in a shimmering lamé gown.

"Sure," he admitted, "I had three wives. All anybody could want."

"You mean *that* was one of your wives?" asked Louie.

Pat peered after the disappearing figure.

"No-o. I didn't say *that* was one. But I've had plenty of them feeding out of my pocket. Not now though – a man of forty-nine is not considered human."

"You've got a cute little secretary," said Louie. "Look Pat, I'll give you a tip—"

"Can't use it," said Pat. "I got fifty cents."

"I don't mean that kind of tip. Listen – Jack Berners wants to make a picture about UWC, because he's got a kid there that plays basketball. He can't get a story. Why don't you go over and see the Athaletic Superintendent named Doolan at UWC? That superintendent owes me three grand on the nags, and he could maybe give you an idea for a college picture. And then you bring it back and sell it to Berners. You're on salary, ain't you?"

"Till tomorrow," said Pat gloomily.

"Go and see Jim Kresge that hangs out in the Campus Sport Shop. He'll introduce you to the Athaletic Superintendent. Look, Pat, I got to make a collection now. Just remember, Pat, that Doolan owes me three grand."

3

IT DIDN'T SEEM HOPEFUL to Pat, but it was better than nothing. Returning for his coat to his room in the Writers' Building, he was in time to pick up a plainting telephone.

"This is Evylyn," said a fluttering voice. "I can't get rid of it this afternoon. There's cars on every road—"

"I can't talk about it here," said Pat quickly. "I got to go over to UWC on a notion."

"I've tried," she wailed, "and *tried*! And every time some car comes along—"

"Aw, please!" He hung up – he had enough on his mind.

For years Pat had followed the deeds of "the Trojuns" of USC and the almost as fabulous doings of "the Roller Coasters", who represented the Univ. of the Western Coast. His interest was not so much physiological, tactical or intellectual as it was mathematical – but the Rollers had cost him plenty in their day – and thus it was with a sense of vague proprietorship that he stepped upon the half DeMille,* half Aztec campus.

He located Kresge, who conducted him to Superintendent Kit Doolan. Mr Doolan, a famous ex-tackle, was in excellent humour. With five coloured giants in this year's line, none of them quite old enough for pensions, but all men of experience, his team was in a fair way to conquer his section.

"Glad to be of help to your studio," he said. "Glad to help Mr Berners – or Louie. What can I do for you? You want to make a picture?… Well, we can always use publicity. Mr Hobby, I got a meeting of the Faculty Committee in just five minutes, and perhaps you'd like to tell them your notion."

"I don't know," said Pat doubtfully. "What I thought was maybe I could have a spiel with you. We could go somewhere and hoist one."

"Afraid not," said Doolan jovially. "If those smarties smelt liquor on me – boy! Come on over to the meeting – somebody's been getting away with watches and jewellery on the campus and we're sure it's a student."

Mr Kresge, having played his role, got up to leave.

"Like something good for the fifth tomorrow?"

"Not me," said Mr Doolan.

"You, Mr Hobby?"

"Not me," said Pat.

4

ENDING THEIR ALLIANCE with the underworld, Pat Hobby and Superintendent Doolan walked down the corridor of the Administration Building. Outside the Dean's office Doolan said:

"As soon as I can, I'll bring you in and introduce you."

As an accredited representative neither of Jack Berners's nor of the studio, Pat waited with a certain malaise. He did not look forward to confronting a group of highbrows, but he remembered that he bore an humble but warming piece of merchandise in his threadbare overcoat. The Dean's assistant had left her desk to take notes at the conference, so he repleted his calories with a long, gagging draught.

In a moment, there was a responsive glow and he settled down in his chair, his eye fixed on the door marked:

SAMUEL K. WISKETH

DEAN OF THE STUDENT BODY

It might be a somewhat formidable encounter.

...but why? There were stuffed shirts – everybody knew that. They had college degrees but they could be bought. If they'd play ball with the studio they'd get a lot of good publicity for UWC. And that meant bigger salaries for them, didn't it, and more jack?

The door to the conference room opened and closed tentatively. No one came out, but Pat sat up and readied himself. Representing the fourth-biggest industry in America, or *al*most representing it, he must not let a bunch of highbrows stare him down. He was not without an inside view of higher education – in his early youth he had once been the "Buttons" in the DKE House* at the University of Pennsylvania. And with encouraging chauvinism he assured himself that Pennsylvania had it over this pioneer enterprise like a tent.

The door opened – a flustered young man with beads of sweat on his forehead came tearing out, tore through – and disappeared. Mr Doolan stood calmly in the doorway.

"All right, Mr Hobby," he said.

Nothing to be scared of. Memories of old college days continued to flood over Pat as he walked in. And instantaneously, as the juice of confidence flowed through his system, he had his idea…

"…it's more of a realistic idea," he was saying five minutes later. "Understand?"

Dean Wiskith, a tall, pale man with an earphone, seemed to understand – if not exactly to approve. Pat hammered in his point again.

"It's up to the minute," he said patiently, "what we call 'a topical'. You admit that young squirt who went out of here was stealing watches, don't you?"

The faculty committee, all except Doolan, exchanged glances, but no one interrupted.

"There you are," went on Pat triumphantly. "You turn him in to the newspapers. But here's the twist. In the picture we make, it turns out he steals the watches to support his young *brother* – and his young brother is the mainstay of the football team! He's the climax runner. We probably try to borrow Tyrone Power, but we use one of *your* players as a double."

Pat paused, trying to think of everything.

"...of course, we've got to release it in the Southern states, so it's got to be one of your players that's white."

There was an unquiet pause. Mr Doolan came to his rescue.

"Not a bad idea," he suggested.

"It's an appalling idea," broke out Dean Wiskith. "It's..."

Doolan's face tightened slowly.

"Wait a minute," he said. "Who's telling *who* around here? You listen to *him*!"

The Dean's assistant, who had recently vanished from the room at the call of a buzzer, had reappeared, and was whispering in the Dean's ear. The latter started.

"Just a minute, Mr Doolan," he said. He turned to the other members of the committee.

"The proctor has a disciplinary case outside and he can't legally hold the offender. Can we settle it first? And then get back to this" – he glared at Mr Doolan – "to this preposterous idea?"

At his nod the assistant opened the door.

This proctor, thought Pat, ranging back to his days on the vine-clad, leafy campus, looked like all proctors, an intimidated cop, a scarcely civilized beast of prey.

"Gentlemen," the proctor said, with delicately modulated respect, "I've got something that can't be explained away." He shook his head, puzzled, and then continued: "I know it's all wrong – but I can't seem to get to the point of it. I'd like to turn it over to you – I'll just show you the evidence and the offender… Come in, you."

As Evylyn Lascalles entered, followed shortly by a big clinking pillow cover which the proctor deposited beside her, Pat thought once more of the elm-covered campus of the University of Pennsylvania. He wished passionately that he were there. He wished it more than anything in the world. Next to that he wished that Doolan's back, behind which he tried to hide by a shifting of his chair, were broader still.

"There you are!" she cried gratefully. "Oh, Mr Hobby – thank God! I couldn't get rid of them – and I couldn't take them home – my mother would kill me. So I came here to find you – and this man packed into the back seat of my car."

"What's in that sack?" demanded Dean Wiskith. "Bombs? What?"

Seconds before the proctor had picked up the sack and bounced it on the floor, so that it gave out a clear unmistakable sound, Pat could have told them. There were dead soldiers – pints, half-pints, quarts – the evidence of four strained weeks at two fifty – empty bottles collected from his office drawers. Since his contract was up tomorrow, he had thought it best not to leave such witnesses behind.

Seeking for escape, his mind reached back for the last time to those careless days of fetch-and-carry at the University of Pennsylvania.

"I'll take it," he said, rising.

Slinging the sack over his shoulder, he faced the faculty committee and said, surprisingly:

"Think it over."

5

"WE DID," MR DOOLAN TOLD HIS WIFE THAT NIGHT. "But we never made head nor tail of it."

"It's kind of spooky," said Mrs Doolan. "I hope I don't dream tonight. The poor man with that sack! I keep thinking he'll be down in purgatory – and they'll make him carve a ship in *every one* of those bottles – before he can go to heaven."

"Don't!" said Doolan quickly. "You'll have *me* dreaming. There were plenty bottles."

Note on the Text

The text in the present edition is based on the collection *The Pat Hobby Stories* (Charles Scribner's Sons, 1962), which compiled the stories published in *Esquire* between 1940 and 1941. The spelling and punctuation have been anglicized, standardized, modernized and made consistent throughout.

Notes

p. 11, *Biograph*: The American Mutoscope and Biograph Company, a major film production company from 1895 to 1928.

p. 20, *It Happened One Night... Hedy Lamarr*: *It Happened One Night* (1934) was a hugely popular screwball comedy directed by Frank Capra (1897–1991). Hedy Lamarr (1914–2000) was a successful Austrian-born Hollywood actress.

p. 22, *Santa Anita*: A famous racecourse in California.

p. 27, *Ronald Colman*: Ronald Colman (1891–1958) was an English actor who was very popular in the US at the time.

p. 56, *Claudette Colbert or Betty Field*: Claudette Colbert (1903–96) and Betty Field (1913–73) were two of the most prominent leading ladies in Hollywood at the time.

p. 61, *the Arbuckle case*: A reference to the highly publicized trials of the film star Roscoe "Fatty" Arbuckle (1887–1933), who was accused of the rape and manslaughter of a young actress, but acquitted in 1922.

p. 67, *Bonita Granville*: Bonita Granville (1923–88) was an American actress. She was best known for a series of films, beginning with *Nancy Drew, Detective*, in which she played the titular sleuth.

p. 72, *Gloria Swanson or Joan Crawford*: Gloria Swanson (1899–1983) and Joan Crawford (1904–77) were major Hollywood actresses.

p. 73, *Stella Dallas*: A reference to the protagonist of the eponymous 1937 film who, despite starting out as a ruthless social climber, finds herself changed by motherhood.

p. 75, *the runner*: A reference to Gene Venzke (1908–92), an American Olympic athlete.

p. 77, *Melvyn Douglas and Robert Young and Ronald Colman and Young Doug*: Melvyn Douglas (1901–81), Robert Young (1907–98) and Douglas Fairbanks, Jr (1909–2000) were popular actors in the 1930s. For Ronald Colman, see note to p. 27.

p. 78, *George Brent*: George Brent (1899–1979) was an Irish actor who enjoyed success in Hollywood in the 1930s.

p. 79, *Upton Sinclair or Sinclair Lewis*: Upton Sinclair (1878–1968) and Sinclair Lewis (1885–1951) were prominent American authors, both of whom espoused left-wing views.

p. 79, *the Wagner Act*: The Wagner Act, or National Labor Relations Act of 1935, guaranteed certain rights to trade unions in the US.

p. 91, *Benchley... and Don Stuart and Lewis and Wilder and Woollcott*: Although the references to "Lewis" and "Wilder" are unclear in this context, Berners is listing people who had prominent careers in other fields before acting in Hollywood productions: Robert Benchley (1889–1945) was a humorist, Donald Stuart (1889–1944) was a London-born screen and radio actor and Alexander Woollcott (1887–1943) was a celebrated critic and raconteur.

p. 100, *Captains Courageous... Mr Smith Goes to Washington*: Pat Hobby is listing some of the most successful Hollywood productions from 1937–39, all written by different people.

p. 102, *Bank Holiday 1933*: Immediately after coming to office in March 1933 in the midst of a major banking crisis, President Franklin D. Roosevelt issued a proclamation shutting down the American banking system. The "bank holiday" lasted for a week.

p. 107, *Mabel Normand and Barbara La Marr*: Mabel Normand (1892–1930) and Barbara La Marr (1896–1926) were among the leading Hollywood actresses of the silent era.

p. 108, *The Trojuns*: A reference to the Trojans, the varsity team of the University of Southern California.

p. 120, *Irvin Cobb*: Irvin S. Cobb (1876–1944) was a famous columnist and author.

p. 133, *mauvais quart d'heure*: "Bad quarter of an hour" (French).

p. 134, *Jack Benny and Baby Sandy and Hedy Lamarr*: Jack Benny (1894–1974) was an American comedian and film actor. Baby Sandy was the screen name of Alexandra Lee Henville (b.

1938), who was briefly a child star in the 1930s–40s. For Hedy Lamarr, see note to p. 20.

p. 134, *Boldini… Reginald Marsh*: Giovanni Boldini (1842–1931) was an Italian portrait painter. Reginald Marsh (1898–1954) was an American painter who was famous for his depictions of New York life.

p. 140, *Eugene O'Brien and Robert Taylor*: Eugene O'Brien (1880–1966) was a popular stage actor at the beginning of the century who then enjoyed success in Hollywood. Robert Taylor (1911–69) was one of the leading men of post-silent-age Hollywood.

p. 140, *Man o' War*: Considered the greatest thoroughbred race-horse of all time, Man o' War enjoyed a spectacular two-year career on the racecourse before being retired to stud, where he sired scores of winning horses.

p. 141, *Connie Talmadge or Bill Corker or Allan Dwan*: Constance Talmadge (1898–1973) was an American silent-movie star. Allan Dwan (1885–1981) was an influential pro-ducer, director and screenwriter. Bill Corker is fictional.

p. 148, *Reginald De Koven*: Reginald De Koven (1859–1920) was an American composer of comic operas.

p. 152, *ASCAP*: The American Society of Composers, Authors and Publishers, a performance-rights organization.

p. 157, *DeMille*: A reference to Cecil B. DeMille (1881–1959) the director of famous Hollywood epics.

p. 159, *DKE House*: Delta Kappa Epsilon, founded at Yale in 1844, is one of the oldest US college fraternities.

Extra Material

on

F. Scott Fitzgerald's

The Pat Hobby Stories

F. Scott Fitzgerald's Life

Francis Scott Key Fitzgerald was born on 24th September 1896 at 481 Laurel Avenue in St Paul, Minnesota. Fitzgerald, who would always be known as "Scott", was named after Francis Scott Key, the author of 'The Star-Spangled Banner' and his father's second cousin three times removed. His mother, Mary "Mollie" McQuillan, was born in 1860 in one of St Paul's wealthier streets, and would come into a modest inheritance at the death of her father in 1877. His father, Edward Fitzgerald, was born in 1853 near Rockville, Maryland. A wicker-furniture manufacturer at the time of Fitzgerald's birth, his business would collapse in 1898 and he would then take to the road as a wholesale grocery salesman for Procter & Gamble. This change of job necessitated various moves of home and the family initially shifted east to Buffalo, New York, in 1898, and then on to Syracuse, New York, in 1901. By 1903 they were back in Buffalo and in March 1908 they were in St Paul again after Edward lost his job at Procter & Gamble. The *déclassé* Fitzgeralds would initially live with the McQuillans and then moved into a series of rented houses, settling down at 599 Summit Avenue.

This itinerancy would disrupt Fitzgerald's early schooling, isolating him and making it difficult to make many friends at his various schools in Buffalo, Syracuse and St Paul. The first one at which Fitzgerald would settle for a prolonged period was the St Paul Academy, which he entered in September 1908. It was here that Fitzgerald would achieve his first appearance in print, 'The Mystery of the Raymond Mortgage', which appeared in the St Paul Academy school magazine *Now and Then* in October 1909. 'Reade, Substitute Right Half' and 'A Debt of Honor' would follow in the February and March 1910 numbers, and 'The Room with the Green Blinds' in the June 1911 number. His reading at this time was dominated by adventure stories and the other typical literary interests of a turn-of-the-century American teen, with the novels of G.A. Henty, Walter Scott's *Ivanhoe* and Jane Porter's *The Scottish Chiefs* among his favourites; their influence was apparent in the floridly melodramatic tone of his early pieces, though themes that would recur throughout Fitzgerald's mature fiction, such as the social difficulties of the outsider, would be

Early Life

Schooling and Early Writings

introduced in these stories. An interest in the theatre also surfaced at this time, with Fitzgerald writing and taking the lead role in *The Girl from Lazy J*, a play that would be performed with a local amateur-dramatic group, the Elizabethan Drama Club, in August 1911. The group would also produce *The Captured Shadow* in 1912, *The Coward* in 1913 and *Assorted Spirits* in 1914.

At the end of the summer of 1911, Fitzgerald was once again uprooted (in response to poor academic achievements) and moved to the Newman School, a private Catholic school in Hackensack, New Jersey. He was singularly unpopular with the other boys, who considered him aloof and overbearing. This period as a social pariah at Newman was a defining time for Fitzgerald, one that would be echoed repeatedly in his fiction, most straightforwardly in the "Basil" stories, the most famous of which, 'The Freshest Boy', would appear in *The Saturday Evening Post* in July 1928 and is clearly autobiographical in its depiction of a boastful schoolboy's social exclusion.

Hackensack had, however, the advantage of proximity to New York City, and Fitzgerald began to get to know Manhattan, visiting a series of shows, including *The Quaker Girl* and *Little Boy Blue*. His first publication in Newman's school magazine, *The Newman News*, was 'Football', a poem written in an attempt to appease his peers following a traumatic incident on the football field that led to widespread accusation of cowardice, compounding the young writer's isolation. In his last year at Newman he would publish three stories in *The Newman News*.

Father Fay and the Catholic Influence

Also in that last academic year Fitzgerald would encounter the prominent Catholic priest Father Cyril Sigourney Webster Fay, a lasting and formative connection that would influence the author's character, oeuvre and career. Father Fay introduced Fitzgerald to such figures as Henry Adams and encouraged the young writer towards the aesthetic and moral understanding that underpins all of his work. In spite of the licence and debauchery for which Fitzgerald's life and work are often read, a strong moral sense informs all of his fiction – a sense that can be readily traced to Fay and the author's Catholic schooling at Newman. Fay would later appear in thinly disguised form as Amory Blaine's spiritual mentor, and man of the world, Monsignor Darcy, in *This Side of Paradise*.

Princeton

Fitzgerald's academic performance was little improved at Newman, and he would fail four courses in his two years there. In spite of this, in May 1913 Fitzgerald took the entrance exams for Princeton, the preferred destination for Catholic undergraduates in New Jersey. He would go up in September 1913, his fees paid for through a legacy left by his grandmother Louisa McQuillan, who had died in August.

At Princeton Fitzgerald would begin to work in earnest on the process of turning himself into an author: in his first year he met confrères and future collaborators John Peale Bishop and Edmund Wilson. During his freshman year Fitzgerald won a competition to write the book and lyrics for the 1914–15 Triangle Club (the Princeton dramatic society) production *Fie! Fie! Fi-Fi!* He would also co-author, with Wilson, the 1915–16 production, *The Evil Eye*, and the lyrics for *Safety First*, the 1916–17 offering. He also quickly began to contribute to the Princeton humour magazine *The Princeton Tiger*, while his reading tastes had moved on to the social concerns of George Bernard Shaw, Compton Mackenzie and H.G. Wells. His social progress at Princeton also seemed assured as Fitzgerald was approached by the Cottage Club (one of Princeton's exclusive eating clubs) and prominence in the Triangle Club seemed inevitable.

September 1914 and the beginning of Fitzgerald's sophomore year would mark the great calamity of his Princeton education, causing a trauma that Fitzgerald would approach variously in his writing (notably in *This Side of Paradise* and Gatsby's abortive "Oxford" career in *The Great Gatsby*). Poor academic performance meant that Fitzgerald was barred from extra-curricular activities; he was therefore unable to perform in *Fie! Fie! Fi-Fi!*, and took to the road with the production in an attendant capacity. Fitzgerald's progress at the Triangle and Cottage clubs stagnated (he made Secretary at Triangle nonetheless, but did not reach the heights he had imagined for himself), and his hopes of social dominance on campus were dashed.

The second half of the 1914–15 academic year saw a brief improvement and subsequent slipping of Fitzgerald's performance in classes, perhaps in response to a budding romance with Ginevra King, a sixteen-year-old socialite from Lake Forest, Illinois. Their courtship would continue until January 1917. King would become the model for a series of Fitzgerald's characters, including Judy Jones in the 1922 short story 'Winter Dreams', Isabelle Borgé in *This Side of Paradise* and, most famously, Daisy Miller in *The Great Gatsby*. In November 1915 Fitzgerald's academic career was once again held up when he was diagnosed with malaria (though it is likely that this was in fact the first appearance of the tuberculosis that would sporadically disrupt his health for the rest of his life) and left Princeton for the rest of the semester to recuperate. At the same time as all of this disruption, however, Fitzgerald was building a head of steam in terms of his literary production. Publications during this period included stories, reviews and poems for Princeton's *Nassau Literary Magazine*.

Ginevra King and Ill Health

The USA entered the Great War in May 1917 and a week later Fitzgerald joined up, at least partly motivated by the fact that his

Army Commission

uncompleted courses at Princeton would automatically receive credits as he signed up. Three weeks of intensive training and the infantry commission exam soon followed, though a commission itself did not immediately materialize. Through the summer he stayed in St Paul, undertaking important readings in William James, Henri Bergson and others, and in the autumn he returned to Princeton (though not to study) and took lodgings with John Biggs Jr, the editor of the *Tiger*. More contributions appeared in both the *Nassau Literary Magazine* and the *Tiger*, but the commission finally came and in November Fitzgerald was off to Fort Leavenworth, Kansas, where he was to report as a second lieutenant in the infantry. Convinced that he would die in the war, Fitzgerald began intense work on his first novel, *The Romantic Egoist*, the first draft of which would be finished while on leave from Kansas in February 1918. The publishing house Charles Scribner's Sons, despite offering an encouraging appreciation of the novel, rejected successive drafts in August and October 1918.

Zelda Sayre   As his military training progressed and the army readied Fitzgerald and his men for the fighting in Europe, he was relocated, first to Camp Gordon in Georgia, and then on to Camp Sheridan, near Montgomery, Alabama. There, at a dance at the Montgomery Country Club in July, he met Zelda Sayre, a beautiful eighteen-year-old socialite and daughter of a justice of the Alabama Supreme Court. An intense courtship began and Fitzgerald soon proposed marriage, though Zelda was nervous about marrying a man with so few apparent prospects.

As the armistice that ended the Great War was signed on 11th November 1918, Fitzgerald was waiting to embark for Europe, and had already been issued with his overseas uniform. The closeness by which he avoided action in the Great War stayed with Fitzgerald, and gave him another trope for his fiction, with many of his characters, Amory Blaine from *This Side of Paradise* and Jay Gatsby among them, attributed with abortive or ambiguous military careers. Father Fay, who had been involved, and had tried to involve Fitzgerald, in a series of mysterious intelligence operations during the war, died in January 1919, leaving Fitzgerald without a moral guide just as he entered the world free from the restrictions of Princeton and the army. Fay would be the dedicatee of *This Side of Paradise*.

Literary   Fitzgerald's first move after the war was to secure gainful
Endeavours   employment at Barron Collier, an advertising agency, producing copy for trolley-car advertisements. At night he continued to work hard at his fiction, collecting 112 rejection slips over this period. Relief was close at hand, however, with *The Smart Set* printing a revised version of 'Babes in the Wood' (a short story that had previous appeared in *Nassau Literary Magazine* and

that would soon be cannibalized for *This Side of Paradise*) in their September 1919 issue. *The Smart Set*, edited by this time by H.L. Mencken and George Jean Nathan, who would both become firm supporters of Fitzgerald's talent, was a respected literary magazine, but not a high payer; Fitzgerald received $30 for this first appearance. Buoyed by this, and frustrated by his job, Fitzgerald elected to leave work and New York and return to his parents' house in St Paul, where he would make a concerted effort to finish his novel. As none of the early drafts of *The Romantic Egoist* survive, it is impossible to say with complete certainty how much of that project was preserved in the draft of *This Side of Paradise* that emerged at St Paul. It was, at any rate, more attractive to Scribner in its new form, and the editor Maxwell Perkins, who would come to act as both editor and personal banker for Fitzgerald, wrote on 16th September to say that the novel had been accepted. Soon after he would hire Harold Ober to act as his agent, an arrangement that would continue throughout the greatest years of Fitzgerald's output and that would benefit the author greatly, despite sometimes causing Ober a great deal of difficulty and anxiety. Though Fitzgerald would consider his novels the artistically important part of his work, it would be his short stories, administered by Ober, which would provide the bulk of his income. Throughout his career a regular supply of short stories appeared between his novels, a supply that became more essential and more difficult to maintain as the author grew older.

Newly confident after the acceptance of *This Side of Paradise*, Fitzgerald set about revising a series of his previous stories, securing another four publications in *The Smart Set*, one in *Scribner's Magazine* and one in *The Saturday Evening Post*, an organ that would prove to be one of the author's most dependable sources of income for many years to come. By the end of 1919 Fitzgerald had made $879 from writing: not yet a living, but a start. His receipts would quickly increase. Thanks to Ober's skilful assistance *The Saturday Evening Post* had taken another six stories by February 1920, at $400 each. In March *This Side of Paradise* was published and proved to be a surprising success, selling 3,000 in its first three days and making instant celebrities of Fitzgerald and Zelda, who would marry the author on 3rd April, her earlier concerns about her suitor's solvency apparently eased by his sudden literary success. During the whirl of 1920, the couple's *annus mirabilis*, other miraculous portents of a future of plenty included the sale of a story, 'Head and Shoulders', to Metro Films for $2,500, the sale of four stories to *Metropolitan Magazine* for $900 each and the rapid appearance of *Flappers and Philosophers*, a volume of stories, published by Scribner in September. By the end of the year Fitzgerald, still in

Success

his mid-twenties, had moved into an apartment on New York's West 59th Street and was hard at work on his second novel.

Zelda discovered she was pregnant in February 1921, and in May the couple headed to Europe where they visited various heroes and attractions, including John Galsworthy. They returned in July to St Paul, where a daughter, Scottie, was born on 26th October. Fitzgerald was working consistently and well at this time, producing a prodigious amount of high-quality material. *The Beautiful and Damned*, his second novel, was soon ready and began to appear as a serialization in *Metropolitan Magazine* from September. Its publication in book form would have to wait until March 1922, at which point it received mixed reviews, though Scribner managed to sell 40,000 copies of it in its first year of publication. Once again it would be followed within a few months by a short-story collection, *Tales of the Jazz Age*, which contained such classics of twentieth-century American literature as 'May Day', 'The Diamond as Big as the Ritz' and 'The Curious Case of Benjamin Button'.

1923 saw continued successes and a first failure. Receipts were growing rapidly: the Hearst organization bought first option in Fitzgerald's stories for $1,500, he sold the film rights for *This Side of Paradise* for $10,000 and he began selling stories to *The Saturday Evening Post* for $1,250 each. *The Vegetable*, on the other hand, a play that he had been working on for some time, opened in Atlantic City and closed almost immediately following poor reviews, losing Fitzgerald money. By the end of the year his income had shot up to $28,759.78, but he had spent more than that on the play and fast living, and found himself in debt as a result.

The Fitzgeralds' high living was coming at an even higher price. In an attempt to finish his new project Fitzgerald set out for Europe with Zelda and landed up on the French Riviera, a situation that provided the author with the space and time to make some real progress on his novel. While there, however, Zelda met Édouard Jozan, a French pilot, and began a romantic entanglement that put a heavy strain on her marriage. This scenario has been read by some as influencing the final drafting of *The Great Gatsby*, notably Gatsby's disillusionment with Daisy. It would also provide one of the central threads of *Tender Is the Night*, while Gerald and Sara Murphy, two friends they made on the Riviera, would be models for that novel's central characters. Throughout 1924 their relations became more difficult, their volatility was expressed through increasingly erratic behaviour and by the end of the year Fitzgerald's drinking was developing into alcoholism.

Some progress was made on the novel, however, and a draft was sent to Scribner in October. A period of extensive and crucial revisions followed through January and February 1925, with the novel already at the galley-proof stage. After extensive negotiations with Max Perkins, the new novel also received its final title at about this time. Previous titles had included *Trimalchio* and *Trimalchio in West Egg*, both of which Scribner found too obscure for a mass readership, despite Fitzgerald's preference for them, while *Gold-Hatted Gatsby*, *On the Road to West Egg*, *The High-Bouncing Lover* and *Among Ash Heaps and Millionaires* were also suggestions. Shortly before the novel was due to be published, Fitzgerald telegrammed Scribner with the possible title *Under the Red, White and Blue*, but it was too late, and the work was published as *The Great Gatsby* on 10th April. The reception for the new work was impressive, and it quickly garnered some of Fitzgerald's most enthusiastic reviews, but its sales did not reach the best-seller levels the author and Scribner had hoped for.

Paris

Fitzgerald was keen to get on with his work and, rather misguidedly, set off to Paris with Zelda to begin his next novel. Paris at the heart of the Roaring Twenties was not a locale conducive to careful concentration, and little progress was made on the new project. There was much socializing, however, and Fitzgerald invested quite a lot of his time in cementing his reputation as one of the more prominent drunks of American letters. The couple's time was spent mostly with the American expatriate community, and among those he got to know there were Edith Wharton, Gertrude Stein, Robert McAlmon and Sylvia Beach of Shakespeare & Company. Perhaps the most significant relationship with another writer from this period was with Ernest Hemingway, with whom Fitzgerald spent much time (sparking jealousy in Zelda), and for whom he would become an important early supporter, helping to encourage Scribner to publish *The Torrents of Spring* and *The Sun Also Rises*, for which he also gave extensive editorial advice. The summer of 1925 was again spent on the Riviera, but this time with a rowdier crowd (which included John Dos Passos, Archibald MacLeish and Rudolph Valentino) and little progress was made on the new book. February 1926 saw publication of the inevitable follow-up short-story collection, this time *All the Sad Young Men*, of which the most significant pieces were 'The Rich Boy', 'Winter Dreams' and 'Absolution'. All three are closely associated with *The Great Gatsby*, and can be read as alternative routes into the Gatsby story.

Hollywood

With the new novel still effectively stalled, Fitzgerald decamped to Hollywood at the beginning of 1927, where he was engaged by United Artists to write a flapper comedy that was never produced in the end. These false starts were not, however, adversely affecting Fitzgerald's earnings, and 1927 would represent the highest annual earnings the author had achieved so far: $29,757.87, largely from short-story sales. While in California Fitzgerald began a dalliance with Lois Moran, a seventeen-year-old aspiring actress – putting further strain on his relationship with Zelda. After the couple moved back east (to Delaware) Zelda began taking ballet lessons in an attempt to carve a niche for herself that might offer her a role beyond that of the wife of a famous author. She would also make various attempts to become an author in her own right. The lessons would continue under the tutelage of Lubov Egorova when the Fitzgeralds moved to Paris in the summer of 1928, with Zelda's obsessive commitment to dance practice worrying those around her and offering the signs of the mental illness that was soon to envelop her.

Looking for a steady income stream (in spite of very high earnings expenditure was still outstripping them), Fitzgerald set to work on the "Basil" stories in 1928, earning $31,500 for nine that appeared in *The Saturday Evening Post*, forcing novel-writing into the background. The next year his *Post* fee would rise to $4,000 a story. Throughout the next few years he would move between the USA and Europe, desperate to resuscitate that project, but make little inroads.

Zelda's Mental Illness

By 1930 Zelda's behaviour was becoming more and more erratic, and on 23rd April she was checked into the Malmaison clinic near Paris for rest and assistance with her mental problems. Deeply obsessed with her dancing lessons, and infatuated with Egorova, she discharged herself from the clinic on 11th May and attempted suicide a few days later. After this she was admitted to the care of Dr Oscar Forel in Switzerland, who diagnosed her as schizophrenic. Such care was expensive and placed a new financial strain on Fitzgerald, who responded by selling another series of stories to the *Post* and earning $32,000 for the year. The most significant story of this period was 'Babylon Revisited'. Zelda improved and moved back to Montgomery, Alabama, and the care of the Sayre family in September 1931. That autumn Fitzgerald would make another abortive attempt to break into Hollywood screenwriting.

At the beginning of 1932 Zelda suffered a relapse during a trip to Florida and was admitted to the Henry Phipps Psychiatric Clinic in Baltimore. While there she would finish work on a novel, *Save Me the Waltz*, that covered some of the same material her husband was using in his novel about the Riviera. Upon completion she sent the manuscript to Perkins at Scribner, without passing it to her husband, which caused much distress. Fitzgerald helped her to edit the book nonetheless, removing much of the material he intended to use, and Scribner accepted it and published it on 7th October. It received poor reviews and did not sell. Finally accepting that she had missed her chance to become a professional dancer, Zelda now poured her energies into painting. Fitzgerald would organize a show of these in New York in 1934, and a play, *Scandalabra*, that would be performed by the Junior Vagabonds, an amateur Baltimore drama group, in the spring of 1933.

His own health now beginning to fail, Fitzgerald returned to his own novel and rewrote extensively through 1933, finally submitting it in October. *Tender Is the Night* would appear in serialized form in *Scribner's Magazine* from January to April 1934 and would then be published, in amended form, on 12th April. It was generally received positively and sold well, though again not to the blockbusting extent that Fitzgerald had hoped for. This would be Fitzgerald's final completed novel. He was thirty-seven.

Final Novel

With the receipts for *Tender Is the Night* lower than had been hoped for and Zelda still erratic and requiring expensive medical supervision, Fitzgerald's finances were tight. From this point on he found it increasingly difficult to produce the kind of high-quality, extended pieces that could earn thousands of dollars in glossies like *The Saturday Evening Post*. From 1934 many of his stories were shorter and brought less money, while some of them were simply sub-standard. Of the outlets for this new kind of work, *Esquire* proved the most reliable, though it only paid $250 a piece, a large drop from his salad days at the *Post*.

Financial Problems and Artistic Decline

March 1935 saw the publication of *Taps at Reveille*, another collection of short stories from Scribner. It was a patchy collection, but included the important 'Babylon Revisited', while 'Crazy Sunday' saw his first sustained attempt at writing about Hollywood, a prediction of the tendency of much of his work to come. His next significant writing came, however, with three articles that appeared in the February, March and April 1936 numbers of *Esquire*: 'The Crack-up', 'Pasting It Together' and 'Handle with Care'. These essays were brutally confessional, and irritated many of those around Fitzgerald, who felt that he was airing his dirty laundry in public. His agent Harold Ober was concerned that by publicizing his own battles with depression and alcoholism he would give the high-paying glossies the impression that he was unreliable, making future magazine work harder to come by. The pieces have, however, come to be regarded as Fitzgerald's greatest non-fiction work and are an essential document in both the construction of his own legend and in the mythologizing of the Jazz Age.

Later in 1936, on the author's fortieth birthday in September, he gave an interview in *The New York Post* to Michael Mok. The article was a sensationalist hatchet job entitled 'Scott Fitzgerald, 40, Engulfed in Despair' and showed him as a

Suicide Attempt and Worsening Health

depressed dipsomaniac. The publication of the article wounded Fitzgerald further and he tried to take his own life through an overdose of morphine. After this his health continued to deteriorate and various spates in institutions followed, for influenza, for tuberculosis and, repeatedly, in attempts to treat his alcoholism.

His inability to rely on his own physical and literary powers meant a significant drop in his earning capabilities; by 1937 his debts exceeded $40,000, much of which was owed to his agent Ober and his editor Perkins, while Fitzgerald still had to pay Zelda's medical fees and support his daughter and himself. A solution to this desperate situation appeared in July: MGM would hire him as a screenwriter at $1,000 a week for six months. He went west, hired an apartment and set about his work. He contributed to various films, usually in collaboration with other writers, a system that irked him. Among these were *A Yank at Oxford* and various stillborn projects, including *Infidelity*, which was to have starred Joan Crawford, and an adaptation of 'Babylon Revisited'. He only received one screen credit from this time, for an adaptation of Erich Maria Remarque's novel *Three Comrades*, produced by Joseph Mankiewicz. His work on this picture led to a renewal of his contract, but no more credits followed.

Sheila Graham

While in Hollywood Fitzgerald met Sheila Graham, a twenty-eight-year-old English gossip columnist, with whom he began an affair. Graham, who initially attracted Fitzgerald because of her physical similarity to the youthful Zelda, became Fitzgerald's partner during the last years of his life, cohabiting with the author quite openly in Los Angeles. It seems unlikely that Zelda, still in medical care, ever knew about her. Graham had risen up from a rather murky background in England and Fitzgerald set about improving her with his "College of One", aiming to introduce her to his favoured writers and thinkers. She would be the model for Kathleen Moore in *The Last Tycoon*.

Among the film projects he worked on at this time were *Madame Curie* and *Gone with the Wind*, neither of which earned him a credit. The contract with MGM was terminated in 1939 and Fitzgerald became a freelance screenwriter. While engaged on the screenplay for *Winter Carnival* for United Artists, Fitzgerald went on a drinking spree at Dartmouth College, resulting in his getting fired. A final period of alcoholic excess followed, marring a trip to Cuba with Zelda in April and worsening his financial straits. At this time Ober finally pulled the plug and refused to lend Fitzgerald any more money, though he would continue to support Scottie, Fitzgerald's daughter, whom the Obers had effectively brought up. The writer, now his own agent, began working on a Hollywood novel based on the life of the famous Hollywood producer Irving Thalberg.

Hollywood would also be the theme of the last fiction Fitzgerald would see published; the Pat Hobby stories. These appeared in *Esquire* beginning in January 1940 and continued till after the author's death, ending in July 1941 and appearing in each monthly number between those dates.

In November 1940 Fitzgerald suffered a heart attack and was told to rest, which he did at Graham's apartment. On 21st December he had another heart attack and died, aged just forty-four. Permission was refused to bury him in St Mary's Church in Rockville, Maryland, where his father had been buried, because Fitzgerald was not a practising Catholic. Instead he was buried at Rockville Union Cemetery on 27th December 1940. In 1975 Scottie Fitzgerald would successfully petition to have her mother and father moved to the family plot at St Mary's. *(margin: Death)*

Following Fitzgerald's death his old college friend Edmund Wilson would edit Fitzgerald's incomplete final novel, shaping his drafts and notes into *The Last Tycoon*, which was published in 1941 by Scribner. Wilson also collected Fitzgerald's confessional *Esquire* pieces and published them with a selection of related short stories and essays as *The Crack-up and Other Pieces and Stories* in 1945.

Zelda lived on until 1948, in and out of mental hospitals. After reading *The Last Tycoon* she began work on *Caesar's Things*, a novel that was not finished when the Highland hospital caught fire and she died, locked in her room in preparation for electro-shock therapy.

F. Scott Fitzgerald's Works

Fitzgerald's first novel, *This Side of Paradise*, set the tone for his later classic works. The novel was published in 1920 and was a remarkable success, impressing critics and readers alike. Amory Blaine, the directionless and guilelessly dissolute protagonist, is an artistically semi-engaged innocent, and perilously, though charmingly unconsciously, déclassé. His long drift towards destruction (and implicit reincarnation as Fitzgerald himself) sees Blaine's various arrogances challenged one by one as he moves from a well-heeled life in the Midwest through private school and middling social successes at Princeton towards a life of vague and unrewarding artistic involvement. Beneath Fitzgerald's precise observations of American high society in the late 1910s can be witnessed the creation of a wholly new American type, and Blaine would become a somewhat seedy role model for his generation. Fast-living and nihilist tendencies would become the character traits of Fitzgerald's set and the *(margin: This Side of Paradise)*

Lost Generation more generally. Indeed, by the novel's end, it has become clear that Blaine's experiences of lost love, a hostile society and the deaths of his mother and friends have imparted important life lessons upon him. Blaine, having returned to a Princeton that he has outgrown and poised before an unknowable future, ends the novel with his Jazz Age *cogito*: "'I know myself,' he cried, 'but that is all.'"

Flappers and Philosophers

Fitzgerald's next publication would continue this disquisition on his era and peers: *Flappers and Philosophers* (1920) is a collection of short stories, including such famous pieces as 'Bernice Bobs Her Hair' and 'The Ice Palace'. The first of these tells the tale of Bernice, who visits her cousin Marjorie only to find herself rejected for being a stop on Marjorie's social activities. Realizing that she can't rid herself of Bernice, Marjorie decides to coach her to become a young femme fatale like herself – and Bernice is quickly a hit with the town boys. Too much of a hit though, and Marjorie takes her revenge by persuading Bernice that it would be to her social advantage to bob her hair. It turns out not to be and Bernice leaves the town embarrassed, but not before cutting off Marjorie's pigtails in her sleep and taking them with her to the station.

The Beautiful and Damned

The Beautiful and Damned (1922) would follow, another novel that featured a thinly disguised portrait of Fitzgerald in the figure of the main character, Anthony Patch. He was joined by a fictionalized version of Fitzgerald's new wife Zelda, whom the author married as *This Side of Paradise* went to press. The couple are here depicted on a rapidly downward course that both mirrored and predicted the Fitzgeralds' own trajectory. Patch is the heir apparent of his reforming grandfather's sizable fortune but lives a life of dissolution in the city, promising that he'll find gainful employment. He marries Gloria Gilbert, a great but turbulent beauty, and they gradually descend into alcoholism, wasting what little capital Anthony has on high living and escapades. When his grandfather walks in on a scene of debauchery, Anthony is disinherited and the Patches' decline quickens. When the grandfather dies, Anthony embarks on a legal case to reclaim the money from the good causes to which it has been donated and wins their case, although not before Anthony has lost his mind and Gloria her beauty.

Tales of the Jazz Age

Another volume of short stories, *Tales of the Jazz Age*, was published later in the same year, in accordance with Scribner's policy of quickly following successful novels with moneymaking collections of short stories. Throughout this period Fitzgerald was gaining for himself a reputation as America's premier short-story writer, producing fiction for a selection of high-profile "glossy" magazines and earning unparalleled fees for his efforts. The opportunities and the pressures of this commercial work, coupled with Fitzgerald's continued profligacy, led to a certain unevenness in his short fiction. This unevenness is clearly present in *Tales of the Jazz Age*, with some of Fitzgerald's very best work appearing beside some fairly average pieces. Among the great works were 'The Diamond as Big as the Ritz' and the novella 'May Day'. The first of these tells the story of the Washingtons, a family that live in seclusion in the wilds of Montana on top of a mountain made of solid diamond. The necessity of keeping the source of their wealth hidden from all makes the Washingtons' lives a singular mixture of great privilege and isolation; friends that visit the children are briefly treated to luxury beyond their imagining and are then executed to secure the secrecy of the Washington diamond. When young Percy's friend John T. Unger makes a visit during the summer vacation their unusual lifestyle and their diamond are lost for ever. The novella 'May Day' is very different in style and execution, but deals with some of the same issues, in particular the exigencies of American capitalism in the aftermath of the Great War. It offers a panorama of Manhattan's post-war social order as the anti-communist May Day Riots of 1919 unfold. A group of privileged Yale alumni enjoy the May Day ball and bicker about their love interests, while ex-soldiers drift around the edges of their world.

In spite of the apparent success that Fitzgerald was experiencing by this time, his next novel came with greater difficulty than his first four volumes. *The Great Gatsby* is the story of Jay Gatsby, born poor as James Gatz, an *arriviste* of mysterious origins who sets himself up in high style on Long Island's north shore only to find disappointment and his demise there. Like Fitzgerald, and some of his other characters, including Anthony Patch, Gatsby falls in love during the war, this time with Daisy Miller. Following Gatsby's departure, however, Daisy marries the greatly wealthy Tom Buchanan, which convinces Gatsby that he lost her only because of his penuriousness. Following this, Gatsby builds himself a fortune comparable to Buchanan's through mysterious and proscribed means and, five years after Daisy broke off their relations, uses his new-found wealth to throw a series of parties from an enormous house across the water from Buchanan's Long Island pile. His intention is to impress his near neighbour Daisy with the lavishness of his entertainments, but he miscalculates and the "old money" Buchanans stay away, not attracted by Gatsby's *parvenu* antics. Instead Gatsby approaches Nick Carraway, the novel's narrator (who took that role in one of the masterstrokes of the late stages of the novel's revision), Daisy's cousin and

The Great Gatsby

Gatsby's neighbour. Daisy is initially affected by Gatsby's devotion, to the extent that she agrees to leave Buchanan, but once Buchanan reveals Gatsby's criminal source of income she has second thoughts. Daisy, shocked by this revelation, accidentally kills Buchanan's mistress Myrtle in a hit-and-run accident with Gatsby in the car and returns to Buchanan, leaving Gatsby waiting for her answer. Buchanan then lets Myrtle's husband believe that Gatsby was driving the car and the husband shoots him, leaving him floating in the unused swimming pool of his great estate.

All the Sad Young Men

Of *All the Sad Young Men* (1926) the most well-known pieces are 'The Rich Boy', 'Winter Dreams' and 'Absolution'. All three have much in common with *The Great Gatsby*, in terms of the themes dealt with and the characters developed. 'The Rich Boy' centres on the rich young bachelor Anson Hunter, who has romantic dalliances with women, but never marries and grows increasingly lonely. 'Winter Dreams' tells the tale of Dexter Green and Judy Jones, similar characters to Jay Gatsby and Daisy Miller. Much like Gatsby, Green raises himself from nothing with the intention of winning Jones's affections. And, like Gatsby, he finds the past lost. 'Absolution' is a rejected false start on *The Great Gatsby* and deals with a young boy's difficulties around the confessional and an encounter with a deranged priest.

'Babylon Revisited' is probably the greatest and most read story of the apparently fallow period between *The Great Gatsby* and *Tender Is the Night*. It deals with Charlie Wales, an American businessman who enacts some of Fitzgerald's guilt for his apparent abandonment of his daughter Scottie and wife Zelda. Wales returns to a Paris unknown to him since he gave up drinking. There he fights his dead wife's family for custody of his daughter, only to find that friends from his past undo his careful efforts.

Basil and Josephine

Between April 1928 and April 1929, Fitzgerald published eight stories in the *Saturday Evening Post* centring on Basil Duke Lee, an adolescent coming of age in the Midwest, loosely based on the author's own teenage years. A ninth story, 'That Kind of Party', which fits chronologically at the beginning of the Basil cycle, was rejected by the *Saturday Evening Post* because of its description of children's kissing games, and was only published posthumously in 1951. These stories were much admired by both Fitzgerald's editor and agent, who encouraged him to compile them in a book with some additional stories. Fitzgerald did not act on this advice, but between April 1930 and August 1931 he published, again in the *Saturday Evening Post*, five stories focusing on the development of Josephine Perry, a kind of female counterpart to Basil Duke Lee. In 1934 Fitzgerald then considered collecting the Basil and Josephine stories in a single volume and adding a final one in which the two would meet and which would transform the whole into a kind of novel, but he shelved the idea, as he had doubts about the overall quality of the outcome and its possible reception. He was still favourable to having them packaged as a straightforward short-story collection, but this would only happen in 1973, when Scribner published *The Basil and Josephine Stories*.

The next, and last completed, novel came even harder, and it would not be until 1934 that *Tender Is the Night* would appear. This novel was met by mixed reviews and low, but not disastrous sales. It has remained controversial among readers of Fitzgerald and is hailed by some as his masterpiece and others as an aesthetic failure. The plotting is less finely wrought than the far leaner *The Great Gatsby*, and apparent chronological inconsistencies and longueurs have put off some readers. The unremitting detail of Dick Diver's descent, however, is unmatched in Fitzgerald's oeuvre.

Tender Is the Night

It begins with an impressive set-piece description of life on the Riviera during the summer of 1925. There Rosemary Hoyt, modelled on the real-life actress Lois Moran, meets Dick and Nicole Driver, and becomes infatuated with Dick. It is then revealed that Dick had been a successful psychiatrist and had met Nicole when she was his patient, being treated in the aftermath of being raped by her father. Now Dick is finding it difficult to maintain his research interests in the social whirl that Nicole's money has thrust him into. Dick is forced out of a Swiss clinic for his unreliability and incipient alcoholism. Later Dick consummates his relationship with Rosemary on a trip to Rome, and gets beaten by police after drunkenly involving himself in a fight. When the Divers return to the Riviera Dick drinks more and Nicole leaves him for Tommy Barban, a French-American mercenary soldier (based on Zelda's Riviera beau Édouard Jozan). Dick returns to America, where he becomes a provincial doctor and disappears.

The "Pat Hobby" stories are the most remarkable product of Fitzgerald's time in Hollywood to see publication during the author's lifetime. Seventeen stories appeared in all, in consecutive issues of *Esquire* through 1940 and 1941. Hobby is a squalid Hollywood hack fallen upon hard times and with the days of his great success, measured by on-screen credits, some years behind him. He is a generally unsympathetic character and most of the stories depict him in unflattering situations, saving his own skin at the expense of those around him. It speaks to the hardiness of Fitzgerald's talent that even at this late stage he was able to make a character as amoral as Hobby vivid and engaging on the page. The Hobby stories are all short, evidencing Fitzgerald's skill in his later career at compressing storylines that would previously have been extrapolated far further.

The Pat Hobby Stories

The Last Tycoon   Fitzgerald's final project was *The Last Tycoon*, a work which, in the partial and provisional version that was published after the author's death, has all the hallmarks of a quite remarkable work. The written portion of the novel, which it seems likely would have been rewritten extensively before publication (in accordance with Fitzgerald's previous practice), is a classic conjuring of the golden age of Hollywood through an ambiguous and suspenseful story of love and money. The notes that follow the completed portion of *The Last Tycoon* suggest that the story would have developed in a much more melodramatic direction, with Stahr embarking on transcontinental business trips, losing his edge, ordering a series of murders and dying in an aeroplane crash. If the rewrites around *Tender Is the Night* are anything to go by, it seems likely that Fitzgerald would have toned down Stahr's adventures before finishing the story: in the earlier novel stories of matricide and other violent moments had survived a number of early drafts, only to be cut before the book took its final form.

– Richard Parker

Select Bibliography

Biographies:
Bruccoli, Matthew J., *Some Sort of Epic Grandeur: The Life of F. Scott Fitzgerald*, 2nd edn. (Columbia, SC: University of South Carolina Press, 2002)
Mizener, Arthur, *The Far Side of Paradise: A Biography of F. Scott Fitzgerald*, (Boston, MS: Houghton Mifflin, 1951)
Turnbull, Andrew, *Scott Fitzgerald* (Harmondsworth: Penguin, 1970)

Additional Recommended Background Material:
Curnutt, Kirk, ed., *A Historical Guide to F. Scott Fitzgerald* (Oxford: Oxford University Press, 2004)
Prigozy, Ruth, ed., *The Cambridge Companion to F. Scott Fitzgerald* (Cambridge: Cambridge University Press, 2002)